Love and Order

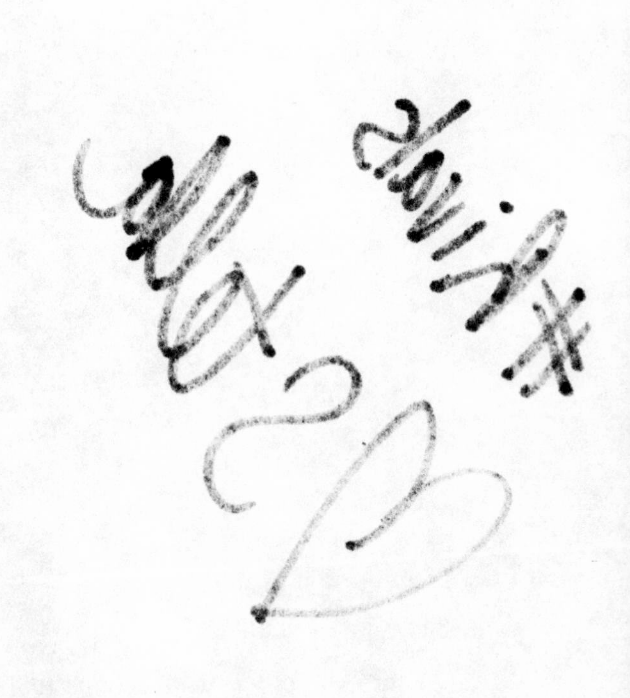

Love and Order

A Legacy of the Maguires Romance

Stella Holt

Love and Order

Tule Publishing First Printing, August 2023

The Tule Publishing, Inc.

First Publication by Tule Publishing 2023

Cover design by Deranged Doctor Design

ISBN: 978-1-959988-85-4

Dedication

For Rachelle.

Chapter One

Finn

WHENEVER THE HAIRS on the back of his neck stood up, Finn knew something was about to happen. It was a cliché he found to be true on every mission he'd ever served on as a SEAL.

Being summoned up to the senior partner's conference room on the fifth floor of the law firm where he worked was his first indication. But now, as he stepped off the elevator into the plush lobby with gleaming slate marble floors and platinum frames wrapped around graphic photos of Lady Justice, he caught the scent of mint. Which could only mean that Hailey Adams was also included in this meeting. His heart skipped a beat, and he could feel a flush of warmth move up his back. Like a childish schoolyard crush, Finn couldn't stop his body's reaction to his colleague—no matter how hard he tried.

Stepping beyond the doorway into the conference room, Finn was rewarded with the sight of her, the most alluring woman he knew—and the most standoffish. She was seated alone on one side of the table, across from two of the managing partners who owned the firm, Mr. Baxter and Mrs.

Stewart. They also oversaw the selection of two rookie lawyers to compete for the coveted junior partner position each year.

"Finn, have a seat, and we'll get started," Mr. Baxter said, gesturing to Hailey's side of the long conference table.

Hailey's back was to him, and her body visibly stiffened before she turned her icy-blue eyes on him, then offered him a curt nod. It was the closest thing to acknowledgement he'd ever received from her. For the two years he'd worked at Baxter and Stewart, Hailey had remained an enigma. Always working, quiet, and by all accounts, the partners' favorite junior lawyer.

"As you may have guessed, this meeting is in regard to the junior partnership," Mr. Baxter announced.

Finn took his seat next to Hailey, careful not to brush her arm draped in a black blazer. Sitting poised with her shoulders back and dainty hands in her lap. The only indication she might be nervous was the light flush that rose along her creamy complexion.

"This year we've decided to try a new model for choosing the junior partner. Instead of giving you each a difficult case, we're pairing you together on a big case." Mrs. Stewart said.

Hailey's breath caught, and he fought the urge to smile. While he didn't have as much time at the firm as several of the other junior associates in the rookie bullpen, since passing the bar, he was by far the more mature option. So this was why Mr. Baxter had been prompting him to be certain about the kind of law Finn wanted to practice long term.

"What is the case?" Hailey asked when neither partner

offered any additional information.

"Good question. We think this has all the markings of a real disaster—a million-dollar empire, marriage in ruins, and child custody," Mrs. Stewart said.

"Child custody? Is this the Tovar *v.* Tovar divorce?" Hailey asked.

"Finn, you better pay attention. Hailey has an uncanny ability to know everything that goes on in this firm. She's already one step ahead of you," Mr. Baxter said.

"Sir, no doubt she is several steps ahead of me, but I run fast, so I'm not worried."

In truth, if he was being put up against Hailey for the junior partnership, it was only a fig leaf to show the other junior associates everyone had to work hard for a coveted partnership. Hailey was dedicated to the law and brilliant. Everyone expected her to be the next rookie elevated to junior partner, but it looked like the partners had one last lesson to teach her.

They each accepted a black file folder Baxter slid across the table to them.

Then the partners stood. "Your first meeting with Mrs. Tovar is in an hour, so you'll need to develop a game plan quickly, as a team. Decide if you'll proceed in court with presenting a united front or allowing one lawyer to take the lead at different junctures," Mr. Baxter said.

Hailey took a deep breath. "To be clear, we'll be judged collectively on the outcome, and one of us will win the junior partnership?"

Mrs. Stewart grinned. Although she'd brought Hailey into the firm, she seemed to push Hailey as much as she pushed herself.

"That's right, Hailey, only one lawyer standing between you and this victory, but you'll have to work with him, not against him. As partners in this firm, we all benefit when we all win, but there is a natural tendency for the junior lawyers to compete or even sabotage each other. The firm can't risk reputation over poor sportsmanship, so we're teaming you together."

"We'll be thick as thieves," Finn offered, but Baxter looked unsure if they could pull it off.

"Good luck to you both."

Once the partners exited, Hailey studied the information in the folder. Internally, Finn was doing his happy dance over the fact that the partners handed him the perfect opportunity to spend time with her. Something he had been unable to accomplish in the two years he'd worked for the firm.

"Finn Maguire. Nice to meet you," he said, facing her profile and perfect posture.

"I know who you are," she said with an exhale while continuing to stare at the documents in the folder. "We have one hour to prep for this, so save the attempts to handle me."

His mouth ached to smile at her seriousness, but he didn't dare. Instead he opened his own folder and began to read. A minute later, he found her flawless forehead scrunched and a frown pulling on her full pink lips.

"Am I missing something? This seems like a cut-and-dried divorce. There is a prenup in place, so Mr. Tovar keeps the majority of his wealth. The custody in the state of Virginia generally favors the mother, but if pressed and able, the father will get 50 percent time," Finn said.

"I agree, but on page three with the full list of assets, it notes that Mrs. Tovar's online retail shop falls under Tovar Enterprises. However, there is no documentation to support that. Mrs. Tovar is specifically seeking counsel on how to extricate her business from the divorce proceedings, but Mr. Tovar is fighting her, claiming a breach of the prenup."

"So the questions are, is the retail shop incorporated under Tovar Enterprises, and who funded it?" Finn said.

Hailey stood. "We need to set up one of the conference rooms on the fourth floor before Mrs. Tovar arrives. Don't forget this is an interview as much as it is a chance for us to figure out what is wrong with this case."

"Not my first year."

She huffed and walked away, leaving him no choice but to follow. She was already in the elevator when he started down the hall. Shoving his hand between the elevator doors before they closed, he stepped inside and took a deep breath. His day just got way more interesting, and the partners had handed him two golden opportunities: a shot at junior partner and the perfect excuse to get to know more about Hailey Adams. But she wasn't going to make it easy.

On the elevator ride down, they were both quiet. No doubt she was considering their case while he was wondering if she was dating someone, but even if she was, it wasn't going to stop him from wanting her. Before arriving at Baxter and Stewart, he never would have believed in the notion of soulmates or love at first sight—he still wasn't convinced. Mainly because Hailey couldn't care less about getting to know him, and he assumed both of those instances required mutual infatuation. But he knew there was something between them, a current of interest that pulsed whenever they were in a room together. Or in the rare instances they accidentally came into physical contact, there was a tidal wave of awareness he'd never experienced, and a blush would spill into Hailey's cheeks, proving she felt it too.

Average height, lean with curves that seemed to defy the loose-fitting suits she always wore. As if she wanted to downplay her figure. Thick blonde hair that looked almost white, which she meticulously kept pulled back. Hailey wasn't a classic beauty but rather a unique compilation of features. A round face, high cheekbones, defined full lips, and unique large icy-blue eyes with one flaw. There was a small facet of brown in her left iris, like ink that spilled into the blue.

He doubted she wore much makeup beyond Chapstick. And if he had to guess, he would bet she'd been a dancer in her early life—the way she carried herself reminded him of a ballerina, each step measured, taking great care to move with purpose. Her eyes were always taking in details, but she rarely offered up opinions. In the rookie bullpen, she was all business.

She was the one woman who had instantly captivated him the moment he saw her. Maybe, that was true for most people who met Hailey. The other men at the firm always attempted to get her attention, but she made it clear she was not interested in mixing work with a personal relationship—especially with one of the other rookie lawyers.

Rookie lawyers were any junior associates at the firm vying for a chance to be invited into the junior partner ranks.

There were always six to ten rookie lawyers in the bullpen, assisting the partners, learning the ropes, and competing against each other. Rookies sat on the third floor with conference rooms on the fourth between them and the managing partners' floor, which was on the fifth floor. There was an extensive law library on the sixth floor where Hailey seemed to prefer to work. The firm sat along the Potomac River in downtown Alexandria, Virginia, only a few blocks from the courthouse. It was a prestigious firm, and Finn knew the only reason he'd been given a position here was because Baxter was a Naval Academy grad and former SEAL, just like Finn. It also didn't hurt that his mother was a local judge.

Following Hailey off the elevator, he didn't miss a few interested looks from the other rookies, pretending to be busy. Her office was at the end of the hall, while his was midway. Before he could grab his laptop, favorite notepad, and pen, Hailey was walking back from her office toward the stairs.

"I'll see you in the conference room in five minutes. Don't expect me to play waitress and lawyer today. We need coffee, water, and something to offer Mrs. Tovar."

"I'll place an order downstairs for some pastries," he said. There was a café on the first floor of their building with a few signature sweets. He just hoped they had a few left.

Ten minutes later, the smell of freshly brewed coffee filled the conference room at the end of the long hallway, which Hailey had selected—it had the best view of the river.

"Assuming she doesn't fire us, we have court tomorrow. Just a simple presentation of our case and request for discovery," Hailey said, not bothering to meet his eyes or acknowledge the platter of croissants, cookies, and chocolates he'd managed to get the café to make during the height of the morning rush.

"Listen, can we at least pretend to be cordial? I'm not your enemy. I'm your partner for the duration of this case."

Hailey stood from her seat, exhaled a big breath, and met his eyes. "I don't like being paired up, and I'm aware that Mr. Baxter favors you."

"And I'm aware Mrs. Stewart favors you, so we're even there."

He wasn't about to admit to her that he knew she was a better lawyer with more years under her belt as a rookie. Or the fact that he wasn't completely sold on the idea of practicing private law.

"The partners said we need to work as a team, and I'm pretty sure we have to win. The easiest way to do both is by getting on the same page," he said.

"Fine, I have more experience debriefing clients, and you can prepare the discovery request, then we can flip a coin for lead in court tomorrow," she offered.

"Deal." Finn held out his hand to shake hers, and for a moment, thought she would reject it. But she gripped his palm with more strength than he would have expected and a jolt of something passed between them. He had a feeling he was going to enjoy this case far more than he should.

✕

AN HOUR LATER, Finn was less sure about how enjoyable

working with Hailey was going to be. Although they'd easily convinced Mrs. Tovar they were the perfect duo to represent her best interests. As soon as they were alone, it was like being in a combat zone and he was taking random fire from the opposing side nonstop.

"We aren't going to use the 'she was the homemaker' defense. For one, it doesn't matter. Per their prenup, Mrs. Tovar isn't entitled to any alimony. But for two, she created her business during their marriage. If we say she wasn't working, then we undermine the creation of her empire," Hailey said.

"I'm just saying we could attempt to stack the deck and throw in the lack of equitable shared duties in running their household and raising their child. Mrs. Tovar should be compensated for that time invested in the building of their family."

"I don't disagree. I just think it will undermine our defense that she isn't asking to circumvent the prenup. She just wants to retain her own, lucrative business and have custody of her son," Hailey said.

Finn stood and took a deep breath. "And if the court disagrees, we'll have missed our chance to argue she is actually owed what amounts to severance pay."

"The courts in Virginia rarely take the side of the spouse that set their careers on hold to raise the family, like it or not. And our client was clear, she doesn't want anything from Mr. Tovar, just her business and her son."

"Alright, we'll play it your way," Finn agreed.

Now it was Hailey's turn to stand, and she checked her watch.

"I have court in an hour. Should we flip a coin to see who takes point tomorrow?"

"Very diplomatic. I was expecting you to offer statistics and case study on why leading with a pit bull female attorney in a contested divorce case is best," he said, trying to lighten her mood.

"I could, but I feel like a coin toss will take less time and has more luck in convincing you I'm the better choice."

Finn laughed and dug a quarter out of his pocket.

"Call it," he said, then flipped the coin up in the air.

"Heads I take point," Hailey said just as he caught the coin and flipped it onto his hand.

She took a step closer and the sun shining through the windows made her blonde hair glow, like an ethereal angel.

He lifted his hand to reveal the tails side of the coin staring up at them.

"Perfect. See you in court tomorrow at eight a.m." She didn't hide the annoyance in her tone and collected her things with vigor.

"Maybe we should discuss the case more this evening," Finn suggested. "We can order food and review our tactics? Then you can make sure I won't embarrass you."

"No need, it will be a short and sweet hearing. We'll declare our plan to fight the plaintiff's claim to Pleasure Inc and request discovery on any and all documentation they have on the business dealings. Then file Mrs. Tovar's request for full-time custody of their son with a fifty-fifty split on all of his educational expenses. Easy day."

"Alright, but I think they are going to make tomorrow more complicated than you expect."

Finally, she met his gaze, and the full power of her sparkling blue eyes were on him. "I agree, they will fight us at every turn, but no amount of prep tonight will change that. So get a good night's sleep and be ready not to blow our case before it even gets started."

"Thanks for the vote of confidence, partner," Finn said to her back as she headed for the door.

THE NEXT DAY in court, Finn took point as planned, and as expected, the plaintiff disagreed with the ownership of Pleasure Inc and the request for full custody of their son. But Finn made one huge error in his request for evidence to support the plaintiff's claims with the inaccurate phrase "full disclosure" when they addressed the judge. The moment the words left his mouth, he knew he'd made a misstep. Disclosure was common and needed, but in the absence of not providing a narrower scope in the request for material, they ran the risk of the plaintiff bombarding them with mind-numbing amounts of paperwork. And that was exactly what had been happening since they returned to the office. Mr. Tovar's lawyers were couriering over every document they had seized or had access to, pertaining to Mrs. Tovar's business and the marriage of eighteen years. The conference room was filled with legal boxes.

"Another box of random documents and knickknacks were just delivered in response to your overboard request for discovery," Hailey said, setting down a huge box on the already-covered conference room table.

If he didn't know better, he'd say there was a smirk on her mouth, but she didn't smile, ever.

"Look, I realized the mistake as soon as it left my mouth in court this morning. I'm sorry. Why don't you take a break while I sift through everything and try to determine what we really need to see?"

Lifting the top off the box, Hailey peered inside. "The problem with that idea is I'd have to trust you to know what will pertain to this case and what won't."

"Ouch, do you ever give anyone a break?" he asked.

"You're still my competition for the partnership, remember? There are no breaks here. For all I know, you requested full discovery with no boundaries to overwhelm me."

"That doesn't make sense. I'm at the same disadvantage, and neither of us will get the partnership if we blow this case."

"Exactly why I plan to go through the contents of every box before moving forward with the plan to argue Mrs. Tovar started this company on her own, with no funds from Mr. Tovar."

"The 'he said, she said' approach is weak. We need proof."

"I know," she said through gritted teeth.

Clenching his mouth shut, he knew there was no arguing his way out of her logic. She was too driven to take a chance on letting him help her with the case. Her plan was to work the case how she wanted and try to sideline him as much as possible. Glaring at her back, he bent forward to lift a surprisingly heavy box off the floor, and his glasses slipped out of his pocket. But the box was too heavy for him to retrieve the glasses without setting down the box on the conference table first. In the moment his back was turned, Hailey moved while holding another box, and the crunching sound of his frames filled the room.

"Oops," she said, shifting the box in her hands to look down under her foot where his now smashed glasses lay. "Do you always keep those on the floor?"

With a deep sigh, all he could do was laugh. His frustration and broken frames were his own fault, and it wasn't fair to blame her. Even if her snarky tone begged him to. The laugh started out sarcastic, but when he found her eyes grow wide with surprise and a faint smile spread on her perfectly pink lips, it turned into an authentic fit of humor. Like when one of his siblings did something idiotic, and they all ended up in gut-busting laughter.

"My brothers would love to see me now," he said as he leaned against the conference room table and wiped his hand over his face.

"They enjoy laughing at your misfortune?"

He nodded and watched as she set her box down then retrieved the broken glasses for him. Handing the once square tortoiseshell frames to him, her delicate finger brushed his palm, and an immediate spark between them had him fighting the urge to hold onto her hand.

"I'm sorry I stepped on them."

"It's my fault. I think I have a backup pair in my office."

She nodded. "Good. I wouldn't want you to miss out on looking through Mrs. Tovar's extensive magazine collection," she said, eyeing the contents of the box he'd set on the table.

He turned to face the table. His heavy box was filled to

the brim with magazines, and hers was filled with feathers in every shade.

"What in the world?" he asked.

"Maybe an almost fifty-year-old woman has a hobby of reading younger women's magazines while making feather boas?" Hailey proposed.

"Or maybe this case is going to be more interesting than we thought," Finn said.

Chapter Two

Hailey

BY EARLY EVENING, Finn sat at the other end of the conference table, wearing his thick, black military-issued glasses. He looked boyish and rugged at the same time if that was possible. She almost felt bad for breaking the other ones. Almost. It wasn't really her fault she'd stomped on them.

After an entire day together, she finally had a chance to study him while his eyes bounced back and forth between two documents. His tawny-brown hair was askew from the numerous times he'd run his hands threw it out of frustration. And his brow was furrowed with concentration, but nothing could mar his gorgeous face.

Finn Maguire was the kind of handsome that caused people to take a second look. Women immediately batted their eyes when Finn walked into a room, and men stood up straighter. Not that better posture could compete with the lines of his square jaw, full firm lips, and green flirtatious eyes. In the rare opportunities she had to look at him without getting caught, he always looked like he was in on a joke no one else knew. Mischief played in his eyes and at the corners of his mouth, until today when she gave him a hard time about messing up in court and as each new box of junk or unlabeled paperwork arrived.

"Do you need a second set of eyes on those?" she asked.

He gave no response as he continued to swing his head back and forth from one document to the other.

"Finn," she said louder.

"What, babe?" he said without glancing up.

She could tell the moment he realized what he'd said, and his shoulders slumped. He set the documents down and pulled off the glasses.

"Sorry, I think my brain is officially fried."

Trying not to laugh, she looked over the latest inventory document sent over from the defense team.

"So you don't call all fellow lawyers babe?"

"No, I don't actually call anyone babe. I don't know why I said that. Too much time around my brothers and their wives probably."

She looked up to see his grimace and enjoyed the view of his muscular frame as he stood to stretch. He'd lost his suit blazer after court, and his business shirt was expertly tailored to highlight his muscular chest and broad shoulders.

"It's seven o'clock," he said, looking at his simple black watch.

His shirt sleeves had been rolled up hours ago to reveal tan skin and light golden hair along his forearms that flexed without him even trying. It was clear his body was ripped under his expensive suits by the way everything fit him so well. He had the kind of strength that indicated a dedication to fitness.

"It'll take us until morning to get through all of this,

which is obviously why they sent so much crap," she said, standing across from him along the wide conference table.

With his hands on his waist, he scanned the room before his eyes landed on her again.

"You think there's some golden ticket buried in all this, and that's why they included so much nonsense? They hope we won't find it in time for tomorrow?" he asked.

"Bingo."

"Which is why you said I shouldn't ask for everything they took from Mrs. Tovar's office."

"Right again."

"Alright, I'm going for a run, and I'll bring back dinner."

"A run?" she said.

"It helps me think. I get distracted when I don't get in a workout."

"You gain energy from running?"

"Yes. If you can't stay late, it's fine."

"Oh no, I'm staying. We just need to get organized."

He nodded. "Is organizing chaos another one of your talents?"

"Something like that." She'd found herself in enough chaotic situations growing up. Learning how to compartmentalize unfortunate circumstances had been the first tool she learned as she bounced from one home to the next in foster care. Staying organized and having very few personal items was the other. The last lesson she learned was how to defend herself and know when to run.

"You okay?" Finn asked.

"I was just thinking I hate running, but that's great if you enjoy it."

"I like the steady push it requires. It quiets my mind to concentrate on my breathing." He stopped a foot away from her. "Why do you hate running?"

"I only run when being chased." Clearing her throat she walked away and grabbed a Sharpie. She opened the next box and looked inside. "Eww."

"What is it?" He moved closer to peer into the box.

It was full of adult sex toys: whips, gags, handcuffs, and leather straps.

"Wow," Finn said.

"They're either messing with us for fun, or maybe they plan to use Mrs. Tovar's personal tastes during extracurricular activities as part of their smear campaign."

"Or both," he said.

His sweet, manly scent wafted around her, and the telltale warmth of a blush moved up her neck. Alone in a room with Finn while holding a box of sex toys was too much for her imagination. Even she could see the inherent sex appeal that was Finn Maguire. But anything beyond professional conduct with a colleague, much less her competition, was a very bad idea. It didn't matter that he had intrigued her for two years or that he was possibly the sexiest man she had ever met. There was no way she could risk everything she'd worked for—the partnership—for a man.

Turning away from him, she closed the box.

"If they can embarrass her enough, they can compel her to agree to mediation," she said.

"Very sneaky, but I can tell your brain needs to mull this over more. I'll be back in an hour. What do you want for dinner?"

"Thai food, always Thai."

"You don't eat other takeout?"

"Sure, but my first choice is Thai—green curry, spicy papaya salad—and get yourself something too."

With a laugh, he left. Would he shower after his run, or would she be forced to smell his sweaty scent the rest of the evening? Kicking off her pumps, she stretched her sore feet. Now a good three inches shorter, she pushed her shoulders back. After writing a quick bold note on top of the box with the sex toys, she moved on to the next one. Once she had each of the boxes labeled with a brief assessment of what was inside, she sorted them.

Boxes with documents on one end of the conference table, those with random knickknacks from Mrs. Tovar's office in the middle, and those with pictures or personal items at the farthest end. She didn't move any of Finn's notes but took a minute to look down at the documents he'd been struggling to decipher. One piece of paper had two paragraphs of written words but the letters were scrambled, like a cryptic puzzle. Only someone with the key could decode it. Finn had jotted down a few possible solutions on another sheet. She never enjoyed word puzzles, but it struck her that if she wanted to hide a piece of evidence, which of the thirty boxes would she put it in?

Before she could explore, Finn returned with a bag of food. His hair looked drenched, his white T-shirt was see-through, and his dark blue shorts clung to his strong, muscular thighs. Her entire body tingled at the sight of him, and she used the edge of the conference table to keep herself standing upright as her knees wobbled.

"Holy crap, you really do have a gift for organizing chaos." Finn looked over each of the three batches of boxes all labeled.

"You're all wet," she said.

"Yeah, it started pouring on my way back. Don't worry, your curry is dry."

He held out the bag to her, but her gaze was stuck on the muscles that looked etched in stone under his T-shirt. His upper arms were accented by several tattoos, and one stretched over his right shoulder down the top of his pec muscle. She couldn't stop staring.

When she didn't take the bag of food he set it on the conference table and took a step closer toward her. Now his delicious scent was mixed with rain and sweat, proving it was possible for him to be even more distracting and enticing.

Clearing her throat she averted her eyes and stepped around him, returning to the boxes of knickknacks.

"I was just looking at that weird puzzle you found. I hope you're actually good at decryption, or we may need to find a cryptology program."

"I'm decent. Did you uncover anything earth-shattering, or are we pulling an all-nighter?" he asked.

"Okay, if you wanted to bury a piece of evidence in discovery, where would you put it?" she asked as she grabbed the box she'd labeled toys and slid it in front of herself.

"In a box of junk or with a million other random documents," Finn said, staring at the fifteen boxes of documents.

"I think I'd bury it in a box of things people wouldn't want to touch."

She tilted the box, and the toys fell forward onto the table. At the bottom of the box was a tan manila folder, almost the same color as the bottom of the box.

"Damn, should I go for another run so you can untangle this entire defense? Maybe I could get you some wine or beer to go with your dinner."

Smiling, she pulled out the folder. "No chance. You have a puzzle to decrypt and we still need to sift through each document to make sure we're not missing anything."

"Well, well, who knew a box of someone's used toys and some Thai food could get you to smile finally."

She'd been avoiding looking at him but couldn't resist now. If his good looks were linked to a power grid, it would be fully charged when he smiled. His green eyes looked like a pool of dazzling emeralds, and a small dimple pushed into the left corner of his cheek through the days' worth of scruff.

"It always sounds sexist to tell a woman to smile more," she said.

Like a pinprick to a balloon, his smile faded and his shoulders slumped.

"Yup, there's the Hailey I know."

"I just mean a guy would never tell another guy to smile more."

"No, but I would tell a guy to loosen the hell up."

Shaking her shoulders, she stood to face him.

"Not quite, but it's a start," he said.

"You must be cold. If you stand around in wet clothes, you could catch pneumonia and get out of court tomorrow."

"I don't get cold, not after the teams."

"What teams?"

"SEALs," he said with a sly smile. "But you knew that."

He walked past her toward the door. "I'm gonna clean up, and then I'll tackle the documents and that puzzle. Don't eat everything."

His commanding voice pushed goose bumps over her arms. Why did the one man to pique her interest in years have to work at the same firm?

Stepping up on her tiptoes, she tried to make out the tattoo that looped over his shoulder and down the right side of his back. Unfortunately, his T-shirt was already starting to dry and was too rumpled.

"You're going to have to ask me," he called out before he exited the room.

"Harrumph," she said and then noticed her reflection in the windows, repeating like a house of mirrors. He'd caught her staring at him. "Damn."

She needed to be more careful while working with Finn. He was her competition, and she wasn't interested in men right now, at least not men she worked with. Although she knew it was an old double standard, when a woman in a law office hooked up with or dated a fellow lawyer in that office, lines got blurred and careers were sidelined. The women were viewed as someone's fling or girlfriend and less like a serious litigator, soon the man's career would move upward and the woman would find herself stuck with less important cases—or worse, relegated to contracts and paperwork. She'd seen it happen during her internships in college and in their firm. She wasn't about to blow all her hard work on a hot guy. Even if he was the most alluring man she had ever worked with, or seen.

In an attempt to distract herself, she opened up the folder and found several documents of incorporation of Mrs. Tovar's business, Pleasure Inc. It wasn't a smoking gun, but it was instantly clear why they'd gone to so much trouble to hide the documents. After washing her hands, Hailey cleared a space for herself to eat on one side of the conference table and another for Finn across from her. She didn't like the idea of having to waste time eating, but they'd both need the sustenance to get through the evening.

Digging through her bag, she checked her insulin levels, which were still okay. After dinner, she may need a dose of self-administered insulin, but she tucked the blue bag away just as Finn walked back in. She could smell soap and his own personal scent that was beginning to seem too familiar. Her thighs pressed together under the table.

"You didn't have to wait for me," he said, setting two bottles of water down between them.

If he noticed the distance between their seats, he didn't comment. She watched as he unpacked the food, placing several containers in front of her, then pulled several more out.

"Are you expecting more people for this meal?" she asked. He'd unpacked a total of eight containers and one pretty purple box.

His megawatt smile looked just as impressive close up. It was safer not to look at him.

"I happen to enjoy Thai food also, and I got a few extra items for you to try. Some things they don't list on the menu."

"How do you know they make them if they don't list it?"

"If you know, you know," he said, shrugging his broad

shoulders.

"Hmmm, obviously you've spent time in Thailand if you know these off-the-menu items."

He nodded and started opening containers. "Eat up. I want to read what's in that folder."

"I'll tell you if you tell me what's in that purple box."

"If you eat your veggies, you can have one." His eyes commanded hers. "And if you tell me why you want to make partner so bad, I'll let you eat all of it."

"Bribery won't work on me. But I'll tell you anyway. I want to be a partner because I deserve it. I have more than double the billable hours than any other junior lawyer, and I handle more cases. I've also been here the longest. I was only passed over last year because a senior partner wanted to give the coveted position to their nephew instead."

"That tells me you like to squash your competition, not why you want to be a partner."

How honest should she be?

"I want to be partner because Baxter and Stewart is a prestigious firm, the security of a guaranteed retirement, percentage of annual proceeds, and power to select cases I want to work on."

"Good answer. And you dislike me because you think my connections to another partner will result in you getting the shaft again this year."

"I don't dislike you. I'm neutral," she said.

"So your plan is to knock this case out of the park while keeping your enemies closer."

"Two birds, one promotion."

"How do you know I won't take the credit when we

win?"

"I assume you'll try."

"You know it's not my fault they chose me as your competition, and you could have done worse."

"Because you have integrity, and I can trust you?"

"Yes. But I can understand after last year why you won't want to believe me. You'll still lump me into the boys' club working against you."

"Probably." She plopped a dollop of rice into her green curry bowl and ate several bites.

The warm, coconut milk concoction with lemongrass and spices swirled in perfect harmony. She hummed.

"Good, huh? I found this place last year."

"How far away is it?"

"Three miles, give or take." He took several bites of his noodle dish that looked like it had enough peppers to light his mouth on fire.

"You ran a mile and a half with that to-go bag full to the brim, and nothing spilled or got wet?"

"Three miles one-way, it's six roundtrip," he said, with a cocky side grin that dazzled her.

He pushed the purple box across the table toward her.

"My reward? I didn't even tell you what you really wanted to know."

"You will, eventually." He didn't laugh or even dare her to contradict him with his steely green eyes. He just glanced at her before continuing to eat.

The feeling of dread her past life always conjured started to creep in, but she pushed it down, focusing on the intricate box. There were faint sketches of flowers on the top folded into the shape of petals. She pulled one, and the box opened to reveal four mini cakes, each intricately iced and decorated.

"We can share these if you tell me why you think you deserve the junior partner slot," she said.

"I'm not sure I deserve it, but it's in my nature to compete. I know I don't want to be anyone's lackey anymore, and I'd rather run my own caseload. I know from my previous career that perseverance usually wins the day, but you have that in spades," Finn said.

"So they pit their two bulldogs against each other for a little sport to see who will win the dogfight."

"You might be the toughest woman I know, but you deserve better than a dogfight." He pointed his chopsticks at her. "Is this how all firms choose their junior partners?"

"In private practice or criminal law, it could be even worse depending on the partners holding the golden ticket. A friend from law school said her firm basically required an oath that each junior partner wouldn't quit or have children within the first five years of making partner. She had to sign an NDA, and there was an unwritten requirement for all female junior partners. I'll let you figure that piece out."

"But life is full of choices. Why would she willingly put herself through that?"

"Student loans, her boyfriend was at another firm, and they couldn't afford to live in the city if she quit."

"So we play their game or go to the public defender's office and work double the hours for more than half the pay."

She laughed until she realized he wasn't kidding.

"That might be an option for you, Maguire, but I'm not

going to spend my life scrimping to save for my piece of the American dream on a public servant's salary. Not to mention the student loans I'm still paying off."

He shrugged. "I may not have student loans, but I paid my way with service in the military and I'm more turned off by the hours than the pay." He eyed her after polishing off his dinner. "You ready to fight over those cakes?"

"I don't have much of a sweet tooth. I'm more of a fruit person." She pushed the box back over to him.

"After years of eating MREs, I learned to appreciate the one piece of chocolate after every meal. Now I'm like a toddler and need a sweetie after I eat my meal."

Unable to resist, she smiled at his honesty.

He took out a white encrusted square with green leaves made out of icing and one ripe red strawberry on top. She watched, riveted. His lips surrounded the cake, and he devoured it all with a moan. Only the strawberry remained, and he stood to lean across the table to offer it to her.

"I don't like fruit on my cake," he said, daring her to let him feed her.

She gulped before opening her mouth to him, it was like he cast a spell on her with his hotness. Everything seemed to slow down, and she watched as his eyes darkened to the color of a stormy sea before he gently set the strawberry on her tongue. It didn't matter that he was careful enough not to touch her. They'd just crossed an imaginary line between professional and personal, a line she'd spent years etching out and struggling to maintain with every hour around him.

Instead of overanalyzing why she'd let that happen, she concentrated on chewing the perfect burst of strawberry in her mouth.

He didn't meet her eyes. Had he felt the odd fissure of connection between them?

Clapping his hands, he broke the spell and started cleaning up his side of the table.

"You finish while I crack this code, and then I say we each tackle fifteen boxes. Whoever finds the most damning information gets to take point in court tomorrow," Finn said.

"That sounds fair."

After wrapping up the rest of her meal, she stowed it in the mini fridge hidden in a cabinet and chose a box at random. Comfortable with the quiet, she slipped into her own thoughts, but focusing on the contents of each document proved to be much more challenging with Finn's muscular form only a few feet away. It wasn't like he was the first attractive guy to work at the firm. Just the nicest, she was surprised to admit.

Most of the rookie lawyers that passed through the firm were cocky, and self-assured to a fault. Until now, she'd avoided getting to know Finn, assuming he would be the same way, or worse, but it was already clear he was disciplined, thoughtful, and a good teammate. It surprised her and would make it more difficult to write him off as the competition.

After only a day partnered with him, she was less intimidated by his connection to the other owning partner of their firm. But his previous life as a SEAL was impressive. It proved his commitment and dedication. The fact that he was nice didn't give her any edge. He was relatable where she could be aloof. Aside from one misspoken word in court, which caused the discovery avalanche, he was poised and charismatic—both great qualities for a successful career in law.

His charm had already worked on her as she wondered if maybe they could work as a team to win the case. Initially, she hated the idea and assumed he would try to mansplain things and bulldoze over her to run the case, but he was too nice to be an arrogant rookie lawyer. In fact, he was almost bashful in his approach on the case so far. Unless he was fooling her and planned to double-cross her later.

From her experience, it was totally possible that Finn was just using her to help him win the case and partnership, even if that was completely out of character for him. She needed to give the partners a reason to choose her over him and not get distracted by the attraction that hung between them. She had worked too long to let her guard down now or let another more junior lawyer take the partnership from her.

The disappointment last year when they selected a junior partner from outside the firm forced her to consider options at other firms. Every big city was filled with cutthroat firms, but back in Virginia Beach, she still had a few connections with several of her professors' firms. If there was one thing she always had, it was a backup plan. It was well known that if a rookie didn't make partner by their fifth year, they were basically invited to find work elsewhere. So this was her last year at Baxter and Stewart if she didn't win.

Chapter Three

Finn

A LITTLE AFTER one in the morning, Finn couldn't focus on the documents in front of him anymore. He'd cracked the coded paragraphs but they had no idea what it all meant. Meanwhile, every few minutes, he would find himself sneaking looks at Hailey's legs, her profile, or her blonde hair piled on top of her head with a pencil. A few strands floated around her and glowed in the light.

"Alright, I vote we each get a few hours of sleep and finish in the morning," he said, breaking the silence.

A yawn escaped her pert mouth, and her eyes looked red. He felt bad for keeping her up; not everyone had developed a keen ability to work without sleep. She looked at her watch and pulled out her phone while he grabbed his things and pretended not to watch.

"I'll drop you off," he said. He knew she didn't drive to work. He'd spent the last two years picking up little bits of information about her, but most of her life remained a mystery.

"Um, I'm good. Just pulling up a car service I usually use when it's late."

The app on her phone looked like it was searching for a driver.

"Hailey, please let me take you home. If you don't, then I'll be forced to sit here until a car arrives and worry you didn't get home safe. Then I won't get any sleep, and I'll be cranky tomorrow."

"The horror," she said, tossing her phone in her bag and picking up her shoes. "Fine, sleep wins. But it's going to be a little out of your way."

"How do you know where I live?" he said, following her out and securing the conference room with all their evidence and case notes safely locked away.

"I do my research."

"Clearly." He liked the idea of her collecting bits of information on him.

Once they were in his car, she rattled off an address in Alexandria, in the main thoroughfare of the city known as Old Town. He was raised in the suburbs of Alexandria but was familiar with the historic downtown. Some streets were filled with shops, other blocks looked like low-income housing, and then there were rows with large, beautiful brownstones. He pulled in front of a coffee shop and parallel parked, then realized she'd fallen asleep.

"Hailey," he said softly. He wasn't sure if he should nudge her, but she was deep in sleep. Surprisingly, she didn't flinch when he gently nudged her shoulder.

"You live in a coffee shop?" he asked.

"I live in an apartment above," she said with a sleepy voice.

"Hence the coffee and treats you bring for the paralegals."

She shrugged. "Thanks for the ride. I'll see you at six?"

"Let's make it six thirty, and I'll pick you up to save time," he offered.

"No, but thanks."

"I'm not being chivalrous. I live ten minutes away. You can get the coffee, and I'll swing by here on my way back to the office."

She huffed.

"You'll be doing me a favor because we both know between now and six-thirty you're going to figure out something from what we read tonight, and we can brainstorm on the car ride."

"Fine, but just this once."

"Deal, see you then." He fought the urge to get out of the car to open her door. Instead, he stayed seated. He doubted she would appreciate the chivalry from a colleague, even if they had crossed several friendly lines in the last twelve hours. She stunned him when she accepted his challenge and let him feed her. No doubt a rare momentary lapse in judgment due to the long hours spent looking at their client's documents.

She retrieved her keys and looked around the area before stepping out and gently closing the door. He waited until she let herself in what looked like a solid door up to her apartment. A moment later, a light in a few of the second-floor windows turned on, but he stayed put.

Who was Hailey, really? At work, she was this polished, fierce, quiet, brilliant lawyer who took the bus or her bike to and from work and lived in a modest apartment above a coffee shop.

Her figure appeared at the window, and she caught him still staring up at her. She didn't wave, and it was tough to see her face in the shadows, but he imagined she was frowning at him so he pulled away.

His place wasn't far from hers by car, but he lived in a modern condo building with a view of the Potomac River from his fifth-floor corner unit. It had high ceilings, wide wood plank floors, and minimal furniture—only the necessities—a big couch, a wall of shelves for his books and no evidence of his former life in the Navy. It wasn't that he didn't have fond memories of his time as a SEAL. It was more like he needed to find out who he was without the Navy or his SEAL trident.

When he left the Navy after six years and too many deployments, he had felt one hundred percent certain it was the right move. He never thought he would miss the familiarity or the discipline the Navy demanded, but after three years of law school on his GI bill and two years as a junior associate at Baxter and Stewart, it was safe to say he did miss the Navy. None of that mattered now. He just needed to get some rest before he was due to be back at work. He wasn't going to let Hailey down or blow this opportunity. Baxter and Stewart likely planned to award Hailey the partnership, but he wasn't going to mail it in and let her win without a challenge.

After setting his alarm, he crawled into bed, hoping the cool sheets and exhaustion would actually let him sleep unlike most nights when he suffered from nightmares of war. As he closed his eyes, the only thing on his mind was the secrets behind Hailey's baby-blue eyes.

The next morning, Finn was surprised to discover he'd actually slept for a solid four hours. Making record time with a quick shower, he dressed in his favorite gray suit with a tie his mom said brought out his eyes. Once he arrived at Hailey's place, he stood outside to wait for her on the sidewalk, and she appeared from the coffee shop with a smile. It felt like a warm ray of sunshine in the cool dimness of early morning.

"Why do I get the feeling you solved this case in the last five hours?" he asked as he held the passenger door of his car open for her.

She had two huge coffees and a large pink box with the coffee shop's logo on it.

"Well, I think I solved a piece of the puzzle. They wanted us to find the incorporation papers because they think it proves from the onset that he was a partner in her now-flourishing business of adult toys."

"I thought she said her business was hospitality focused," he said once he was buckled back in the car and eased onto the empty road. At six thirty, there was virtually no one on the road yet, and he knew the drive to the office would take only fifteen minutes. He wanted to maximize that time with Hailey.

"I did some digging last night and learned Mrs. Tovar's hospitality business is in fact a major player in the sex toy industry. She has contracts throughout the US and Europe, and one of her inventions has been the number-one-selling item for women for five years."

"Wow. Why didn't she tell us? She had to have known

this was going to come out in court."

"I don't know, but we can ask her this morning before court. She's meeting us at eight," Hailey said and pursed her lips before letting out a breath.

"Did you sleep at all?" he asked.

"Sleep is overrated, but yes. I got about four hours."

"So our working theory is Mrs. Tovar doesn't need or want half of Mr. Tovar's wealth, which per the prenup she isn't entitled to, but Mr. Tovar wants to keep all his money and get half of hers?"

"Correction: I think he wants to take her business and leave her with nothing. Now we just have to prove it. I hope you don't blush too easily, because I think it's going to get a little saucy in court today," Hailey said.

Glancing over, he caught a faint smirk on her face and reached for his coffee. He didn't miss her hip pull away from his hand.

"Look, you don't have to tell me, but if someone is still hurting you, I'd be happy to see that they never get near you again."

It took effort to keep his tone even and he couldn't see her face while he was driving.

"Old habits, that's all."

He took a long pull on the coffee, letting the hot brew stop him from cursing. His hunch had been right. Someone had done enough damage to Hailey that her natural instincts had been trained to avoid any physical contact and expect the worst from people.

"Are we going to flip for lead in court today?" She changed the subject.

"No chance. You won it fair and square, but I have a feeling Mr. Tovar and his lawyers are going to use intimidation and crass tactics to try to embarrass our client and us."

She nodded. "I can handle them."

He wasn't so sure, but he was willing to stand behind her and let her try. Maybe facing bullies in court was her therapy for dealing with her own history.

An hour later, they mapped out the sequence of events for Baxter, as he and Mrs. Stewart were keeping tabs on them to ensure the case didn't go off the rails.

"Well done, you two. Don't let your guard down in court, though. There may still be more to this puzzle. Most divorces get ugly, but divorces with this much money involved always get nasty," Baxter said. "Finn, will you be the lead in court today?"

"No, sir. I will," Hailey piped up. "We think we can lure the plaintiff into a trap. They'll assume they can embarrass me when they bring up the topic of a sex toy conglomerate in open court. And they already know our client has enjoyed the anonymity of using front companies to run her business since its inception. They want to take us by surprise, and they'll be wrong. We think if I lead, we can turn the tables on them more easily."

Mr. Baxter smiled and nodded. "Very good." Before he dismissed them, he gave Finn a warning look but said no more.

Once they were back in the elevator, they both let out a deep breath.

"You know what that look meant?" she asked.

"Yes, it means if I don't watch out, you'll steal this promotion from me without breaking a sweat," he said.

"I can't steal what's already mine."

He laughed, but as they passed the rookie lawyer bullpen, several of the men smirked at him. They all ogled Hailey as she walked by, ignoring them. The urge to destroy them all surged, but that wasn't an acceptable response. His impulse to protect Hailey was not going to help him get her attention in the right way. She didn't want someone to fight her battles, that was clear.

Inside their war room, Hailey did an about-face with her arms over her chest.

"I don't need your pity. I don't want you to go easy on me because of some misplaced chivalry either."

"What are you talking about?"

"You let me just run the show with Baxter and didn't even fight me on taking point today."

"Hailey, I concede that you've figured out more of this case than I have at this point. I also think letting you take the lead will fool the plaintiff into thinking we don't know their plan. And I don't pity you. I admire you, even though you like to give me shit every chance you get. You're an exceptional lawyer. But I'm taking point with Mrs. Tovar because I don't appreciate her lying to our faces. We're her lawyers, and she could have embarrassed us in court today."

Dropping her hands, she turned away from him. "Fine. You deal with the client, and I'll handle her husband's team."

"For today. I'm not giving you all the glory."

After an hour of arguing with Mrs. Tovar, Finn managed to get her to understand the importance of not hiding anything from the judge or her legal team. Unexpectedly, Mrs. Tovar hoped to keep the fact that she built a lucrative sex toy empire quiet, but they explained that was likely going to be impossible. Then they all went over their plan for court. This hearing was only the beginning, where each party would outline their defense, why mediation was not an option, and the judge would decide if there was enough evidence to go to trial. Assuming that happened, he and Hailey were going to face weeks of working together. He couldn't decide if that was exciting or torture. But he knew any time with her was better than none. It was just going to test his ability to remain professional and not flirt with her.

Before they left for court, Hailey excused herself and disappeared for ten minutes. When she returned, she looked pale.

"Hey, are you feeling okay?"

"I'm fine. Don't fuss over me. We're coworkers, nothing more," she said under her breath so their client wouldn't overhear.

Putting on his suit jacket, he clenched his teeth together. Not that he had a good retort. She was, of course, right again.

In the hall outside the civil D.C. court, he spotted Mr. Tovar in an expensive suit, looking every bit the smug millionaire. Mrs. Tovar had her face in her phone and ignored him. Hailey was chugging a juice box he assumed she'd had in her bag. Maybe a pre-court ritual.

"It's time. This way," Hailey said, ushering Mrs. Tovar to their side of the court. It wasn't until they were all settled at their table and the bailiff arrived that a young man was brought into court and sat on Mr. Tovar's side.

"What the heck is Timothy doing here?" Mrs. Tovar said in open court to her soon-to-be ex-husband.

Mr. Tovar just smiled and told his son to stay put.

The young man waved at his mom with a meek smile and shrugged.

"This is not okay. Our son doesn't know what my business is, and he'll be mortified," Mrs. Tovar whispered to them.

"He is trying to break you," Hailey said in a calm but unfeeling voice. "Do you want to cave and give him half, or should we proceed?"

Mrs. Tovar's hand stretched over her forehead, her cheeks were red, and her breathing was heavy.

"It's not really about the money, Mrs. Tovar. If you give him half now, he'll always have a hand in your business. All the work you've done, any creative decisions, he'll own half of all of it. You'll never be able to get out from under his domineering presence," Finn said in a low soothing tone.

Tears welled in the woman's eyes. "I suppose this is one way to have a conversation about the birds and the bees. I'm just worried my son is going to be pulled through the mud."

"Your son is twelve. As soon as court is called to order, I'll request a sidebar with the judge to highlight the child in court. Your husband's lawyers know the judge won't permit him to stay, they are just trying to get in your head," Hailey said, jotting down a note.

"Thank you," Mrs. Tovar said.

For the next thirty minutes, Finn was spellbound. He was all but useless as the judge sided with Hailey on the removal of the twelve-year-old from the courtroom. The judge then admonished the opposing attorney for even considering trying to expose the young man to his parents' contentious divorce. Next she presented their case and even submitted into evidence the sales reports for Mrs. Tovar's last two years of business and tax records, letters of incorporation, and annual reports on the ownership and management of the company, none of which included Mr. Tovar. The defense attempted to rattle Hailey by bringing up specific details about the sex toys and their concepts that they alleged were developed jointly between the couple. Hailey didn't flinch.

"I could talk about making a Beef Wellington all day long, but it would take a real chef to execute the meal," she retorted.

Finn stifled a laugh behind a cough, but Mrs. Tovar grinned from ear to ear.

Her articulation of the law and detailed knowledge of precedence was exacting and irrefutable. The judge seemed to agree and set the trial date for three weeks later. But when they exited the courthouse, there were news crews shouting questions to Mr. and Mrs. Tovar about their sex toy kingdom. The salacious questions were all asked in front of their son Timothy, and any hope Mrs. Tovar had of telling her son on her own terms was gone. She tried to shield him from the cameras and talk to the young man, but Mr. Tovar took a hold of their son's arm.

"Your court appointed time with our son is next week. Don't make me take you to court for violating the custody agreement in place," her soon-to-be ex barked as he pulled their son away.

"Sorry, Mom," the Tovar's son yelled as he was pulled down the sidewalk outside the courthouse.

"Never get married, and never give anyone the power to hurt you with your own child," Mrs. Tovar said to them both as she put on her dark sunglasses and walked away toward her own car service waiting for her at the bottom of the court steps.

"I don't plan to," Hailey muttered.

"Shit, I need a drink after that."

"Agreed."

He was surprised she was willing to spend time with him that didn't pertain to their case but suspected it was all part of her bigger plan. But any chance to spend more time with her outside of the office was a win, so he was happy to play along.

They walked toward the trendy bars and restaurants along the river walk, and Finn considered his options. Should he bow out of the case and let Hailey handle it? She was more than qualified. But then he would have to admit to Baxter he was having second thoughts about practicing private law, which he wasn't sure he was ready to do. Worse, if he did step away, would they assign another rookie to work with her? He assumed he had another year or two in the rookie bullpen before he had to decide whether he was cut out for private practice or if he needed to try something with more grit. Although after today, private practice was looking grimier than expected.

"There's a good spot just one more block away. Do you like whiskey?" she asked.

According to his watch, it was only ten thirty in the morning.

"Have you met an Irishman that doesn't?"

He followed Hailey's lead into what looked like a hole-in-the-wall, with a heavy steel door and no sign other than the address.

"Is this where you have me killed and secure your promotion?"

"That would take all the fun out of beating you."

Once the door closed and his eyes adjusted to the dim lighting, he took in the high ceilings, leather lounge chairs paired at tables made from big wooden casks, and brass piping running along the tops of the walls. A floor-to-ceiling glass room sat behind an intricate bar, where large vats of whiskey he presumed were made.

"If the whiskey is half as good as the ambiance, I'll have to bring my brothers here," he said.

"How many siblings do you have?"

"I have two brothers and one sister. Charlotte's in New York, but my brothers are both local. Do you have any siblings?"

"Nope." Leaning against the bar, Hailey ordered them each a pour of what they called Number 87 and two cheeseburgers with the works.

"Did you have to try eighty-seven whiskeys to figure out which one was your favorite?"

"I've probably sampled all of their whiskeys, but number ninety-one is my favorite."

"I don't think you'll like it. It's on the mellow side."

"I like mellow, sometimes." He cringed knowing he

sounded cheesy, but something about her made him willing to be a complete fool, if necessary, just to get her attention. Maybe he should ask her if she wanted him to step down from the case, especially if his heart wasn't interested in the partnership. But he wasn't willing to give up the next few weeks of time with her. He was just going to have to decide what he wanted before the partners selected a partner.

The bartender sat their whiskeys down, neat. He held his up to inspect the amber color, and then waited for her to pick up her glass.

"To making partner," he said.

She clinked her glass against his and took a sip. The smokey sweet scent filled his nose, and he tasted the faint honey mixed with citrus and smooth finish.

"Quick, tell me something you're not good at. I'm starting to feel inferior," he said.

With a faint smirk she moved away from the bar to a small courtyard beyond the glass room, its walls covered in ivy. He followed her toward the table farthest away from any other patrons, and they each took a seat. She didn't seem to notice the attention she attracted while walking through the bar. Even now as she sat with him, several others looked over.

"I'm not a great cook," she said. "I can hardly boil pasta."

Smiling, Finn tried to imagine her barefoot in his kitchen and had to adjust in his seat. The vision didn't include her cooking.

"What about you?"

"You already know I don't like to lose, but since it

doesn't happen often, I'm not very gracious when it does," he said.

"Give me an example."

"Alright, several of my family members have cabins up at Lake Anna. Have you ever been?"

"No."

"It's only a few hours' drive but feels like a world away. No traffic, small town, big lake, lots of great hiking, and quiet."

"Sounds like bear country."

"Maybe a few. Anyway, every year we all meet up there and do our annual family relay race. The teams are always different, and it never mattered if I were paired up with my sister or brothers. My team always won. One year, they even made me tie my hands behind my back for the swim."

"Very impressive, but since you're a SEAL, I sort of expected that."

"Right, then last year, something went wrong. The teams had grown, with my sister Charlotte getting married, then Rory, and now Conner."

"So the new people have thrown off your game?"

"Even worse. We did siblings versus spouses, and they annihilated us. It was pathetic. I've never heard my sister curse so much, and it gave their spouses such bragging rights. None of us can wait until this year when we can redeem ourselves."

"Was it rigged? Are your siblings whipped, or did they all marry SEALs?"

"You know, if I hadn't seen it with my own eyes, I wouldn't have believed it. And yes, Conner especially because it's still newish. He is a total pushover for his fiancée. That's my dad's fault."

"Your dad competed?"

A server dropped off their burgers with waters, and he found something else to like about Hailey. She liked to eat. Picking up her burger, she took a huge bite and groaned. He noticed she'd been nursing her whiskey, but maybe she knew she needed something to eat first. Smiling, he dug into his burger before she prompted him to continue his story.

"It's my dad's fault my brothers are such devoted saps. My father set a high bar for his sons, to be men with integrity and total wimps with their wives."

"So your mom runs the show."

"For sure. I mean, they're a team, but she calls the shots. Why are you letting me ramble so much about my family? Why did you agree to have lunch and a drink with me?"

For the first time, a shadow of doubt fell across her face.

"I just, uh, appreciate you not fighting me every step in this case. I admit I thought you were going to be terrible to work with. And I was hungry." Her gaze lingered on him, and he wondered if there was something more she wanted to say.

Leaning forward, he focused on her eyes and tried not to notice the wisp of blond hair that had slipped out of her tight bun.

"It's my pleasure to get to learn from you, Hailey. I knew you were going to be annoyingly impressive, but you have exceeded my expectations—which I will deny if anyone asks."

A slow smile spread her plump lips, and her cheeks

turned the faintest shade of pink.

"Should we get together tomorrow to map out our plan of attack?" he asked. He didn't want to have to wait until Monday to see her again.

"I have plans tomorrow but will be in the office Sunday to work on another case. If you want to come in the afternoon, we can review what we have. I think we really need to study the financials and determine what, if any, funding came from joint accounts and dig up as much precedent on that," she said, between nibbles of her fries.

"How did you rattle off so much case law today?"

"I have a great memory, some would say photogenic, even though that's not real."

"Did you grow up in Virginia?"

"Nope."

"You don't want to talk about it?"

Shrugging, she took another sip. "Not much to say. I grew up in North Carolina. I went to a state college in Virginia, then law school. I finagled a position with Baxter and Stewart because Inez Stewart went to school with my mentor at law school."

"Maybe one day you'll tell me about where you got that grit, but only if you want to." He polished off his drink and stood. "Shall we head back to the office?"

"You go ahead. I'll be there in a little bit."

Disappointment was like an unexpected tidal wave crashing over him, but she'd already spent more time with him in two days than she had in two years. If he was going to convince her to consider a personal relationship, he was going to need to be patient with her.

"Thanks for the drink and lunch. Well done today," he said.

×

LATER THAT AFTERNOON, he noticed when Hailey returned to the office, but they didn't discuss their case the rest of the day. They each had an existing case load, and he picked up on her need to concentrate from her office door being closed. The rookie bullpen always got a little noisy on Fridays, and several of the other lawyers were vocal about planning their evening out. They were all younger than him by at least five years, but usually kind enough to invite him if they were just going to a local bar. But he knew they'd be hitting the trendy club scene, and that wasn't really his style. By six o'clock, he was ready for a run and an early night. Hailey's door was still closed, so he settled for sending her a short message via their interoffice chat system.

I'm heading out, see you Sunday around 1.

He waited, staring at the little box for their chat and was struck with how eager he was for her to respond.

Finally, three words popped up.

See you Sunday.

Short and sweet, and a little underwhelming, but it wasn't reasonable for him to expect her to want to celebrate their success in one pre-trial hearing with him on a Friday night. She probably had plans with someone outside of work. She probably had an entire big life outside the office, some man that spoiled her, friends she brunched with, and didn't give him a second thought. Shutting down his computer, he grabbed his bag and turned off his office light. With one last look down the hall where Hailey's office door remained closed, he made his way toward the elevator. Once inside, he caught his own reflection and smiled. He may not get to see her socially yet, but he still had Sunday and that was a start.

Chapter Four

Finn

THE GLOW FROM the desk lamp bounced off Hailey's glasses while she reviewed her notes and scanned something on her screen. It was only noon on Sunday, and she had the office all to herself.

"So this is how you memorize all those case files?" Finn asked.

Her screech caused a ripple of caution to slide down his spine, like a warning. Her head popped up, and she pulled out her earbuds as the papers on her desk cascaded to the floor.

With his hands up in the air, he cringed. "It's just me, Finn. Sorry."

She stood now with her face in the shadows, one hand on her chest and the other gripping a round object, as if she could fend off some intruder with what looked like a paperweight. Her pupils had grown big in her searching glacier-blue eyes.

"I'm sorry. I didn't mean to scare you."

He took a tentative step closer and watched as realization sank in and her breath started to steady. He bent to pick up the documents and set them on the side of her desk but didn't dare move closer to her.

"You shouldn't sneak up on someone like that."

"I promise I wasn't sneaking. I figured if you were here, you'd have heard the elevator ding, or my laugh when I spotted you working on the case without me."

She looked beyond him down the hall.

"You're early," she said, checking the time on her watch. "I wasn't expecting you for another hour or so. Usually, I have the office to myself all day."

"You mean you come here every Sunday? Were you working yesterday too?"

Squinting, she pulled off the large glasses he noticed she used only with the computer.

"Maybe. Why are you early?"

"I had a thought about something and wanted to look up a case file," he said, holding back a laugh. She was flustered. He held up a bag of sushi. "And I brought us a snack."

"Look who else was working on our case," she quipped.

"Ha, I could have been working on our case all weekend and likely wouldn't be able to keep up with you."

He retreated back down the hall to his office and sat his things down. Each junior lawyer was afforded a small room with no windows, and just enough room for a desk, a chair, and narrow bookcase. The doors were all fogged glass, giving them no ability to see each other or a partner approaching. He waited eager to see if she would follow him and admit he was excited when she joined him in his space.

"Which case file?"

"That's the problem. I can't remember the names of the

case, but it was a big story around here when I was in high school. Did you eat yet?"

"Because?" She drew out the S, in a singsong tone, as if she had to coax him into sharing more details.

He logged into his computer and pulled up the database with all the precedence files in Alexandria, state court. He typed a few key words into the search bar, hit enter, and let the system do its work. Headlines scattered on his screen.

"You can stand on this side if you want to see what I'm looking up."

She moved next to his desk where she could see his screen but was still over an arm's length away from him. It seemed like progress, considering she was ready to beat him up with a paperweight a few minutes ago.

"Love triangle, scandal in the suburbs?" She read the headlines with her glasses back in place.

"There was this couple. They owned all the dry cleaners in my neighborhood, but the husband's girlfriend tried to off the wife, assuming he would get to keep all the cleaners. It turned out the wife had been the business-savvy one, and everything was in her name. The wife survived, and her lawyer proved in court that none of the husband's money had been used in the startup of the businesses. He got nothing in the divorce."

"Very tawdry; I can see why that would get stuck in your brain."

He looked at her with mock disdain. "The thing is, the husband's family was filthy rich so the assumption was he'd used his money to start the businesses but for tax purposes put everything in the wife's name. But the wife proved how she started the businesses and grew her own fortune."

"So if we can figure out how they delineated between funds for the family and funds to start their business, we can use it as precedence," she said, filling in the blanks.

"And likely find dozens more like it."

She grunted, but her lips quirked in a faint smile. Before he could dwell on it, her stomach growled.

"Sounds like you forgot to eat, which seems unlike you."

Backing away, she looked at the simple digital watch on her delicate wrist, and from his angle, he noticed a jagged scar for the first time. She was wearing loose fitted black slacks and a white button-down collared blouse. Professional, but the most casual he'd seen her dress at the office in the almost two years he'd been there.

"I've been digging into the financials. The business didn't start with a loan or a large sum of money transferred from any of their joint accounts. It's like she walked into a bank with a pile of cash and used it to create new accounts from thin air. Fifty thousand dollars."

He nodded, looking at the blank white wall to his right. "Mrs. Tovar said she used an inheritance to start the business. Money from a dead aunt's estate that she technically didn't have to share with her spouse, per state law."

"Right, but it was fifty thousand in cash deposited with no trail. The lawyer that handled the estate is no longer practicing, and she can't find the one letter she received, notifying her of an inheritance. If there aren't any receipts, how do we prove that Mr. Tovar is lying? He claims she used his money, or he knows she can't prove where she got the money from," she said. "We just have to keep digging, and I think you're going to have to grill our client again about all the facts of this case."

"Damn, that woman is making it really difficult to defend her. It's just like they said in law school," he said.

"What?"

"Everyone is lying," he said, meeting her eyes and holding their stare longer than necessary. But he didn't know what she might be lying about.

"I guess we know what we both need to work on today. You find that case file, and I'll continue to hunt through all the finances."

"Sounds like a plan. I'll let you know if I find anything," he said. "Take some sushi back with you." He pushed the bag toward her and watched her hesitate.

Hailey's blond locks looked thick piled up on her head, but several wisps had escaped and a pencil was poking out of the top. She looked sexy and cute, but he wasn't going to tell her that.

"You don't have to feed me." She peeked into the bag.

"No, but a hungry Hailey isn't going to be as effective as a well-fed one, so take any that look good to you. I got a variety."

She selected a tray of spicy rolls and a pair of chopsticks. "I'll buy our next lunch."

"I'm not keeping track, but I'll let you take me out if you insist."

Her eyes narrowed before she turned to leave, and he watched as her hips swayed. She floated out of the room, leaving a hint of mint and something sweet behind.

Then he started searching his computer for the court case

he wanted. He wasn't sure how long he'd been sifting through legalese when his phone started vibrating again in his pocket. His brothers had started texting him, and he realized he'd been in the office for almost four hours. He and Hailey had exchanged a few messages via their work chat system but otherwise were each digging through files. He'd found the case he remembered, but most of the files had a lock attached to them, so he wasn't able to access everything.

Looking up, he heard her footsteps before she appeared in the doorway.

"I'm going to head out for the night. I still didn't find any link between any of Mrs. Tovar's accounts and the business accounts." She sighed. "We can pick up on this tomorrow and request our client give us more details about her dead aunt. Maybe another relative kept better records of the inheritance."

"Hey, real quick. Do you know what this lock next to a file signifies?"

Moving closer, she squinted at his computer. "Sensitive and compartmented."

"Sensitive and compartmented by whom?"

"It means there was some level of government involvement. Could be they were under investigation by the IRS for tax evasion."

He hit print on the document and shut down his computer then stood.

"Want to find out what it was?" Finn asked, hoping she didn't have other plans.

She tilted her head and studied him. "That feels like a trick question but yes. But we'll have to file a request with the court tomorrow."

"Or we can ask someone who served as a district attorney in Alexandria when this case was tried."

"Who?" she asked, her interest clearly piqued.

"Come with me to dinner, and I'll introduce you."

"You have a date for dinner with a district attorney working in the Virginia courts, and you're inviting me to tag along?"

"No, I'm having dinner with my mom, and she was a district attorney in Alexandria when this case was on trial. Now she's a judge."

"Your mother is a judge?"

He moved past her, careful not to touch, but he still took a subtle inhale to catch her scent. Did she taste as delicious as she smelled?

"I thought you did all your research on me and knew that," he said, grabbing the printed documents and heading out of his office. "Shut that door, will ya?" he called when he was halfway to the elevator. Not waiting to see if she would follow, he pressed the button.

The elevator doors popped open, and he held the door for her, then pushed the button for the garage level once they were both in. He knew she usually walked to the Metro. She would need to take the first floor to exit to the street if she wasn't going to join him for dinner, but she hadn't pressed the button yet. Hailey was like a wild animal living in a busy city: suspicious of people. The only option was for him to be patient and wait for her to decide she could trust him.

"I doubt your mom wants to talk about a ten-year-old case over dinner."

She reached forward and pressed the number one. His heart sank, and his momentary disappointment cost him precious seconds on a game plan to convince her to join him.

"My mom loves to talk about law anytime and anywhere, especially with hungry young lawyers. Same as my dad."

"Your dad is a lawyer too?"

"No, retired cop."

"So you're having dinner with your parents?"

"Technically, it's a standing Sunday family dinner, and I'm late." The elevator dinged for the first floor, and he held the door open for her. "If you come with me, we can pick my mom's brain on the case study."

"I don't think it's a good idea."

"You're so hungry you can't think straight. Come on, do me a favor."

She eyed him with her sparkling sapphire eyes. "How is bringing a stranger to your family dinner doing you a favor?"

"Well, for one, my mom is a great cook, so I'll win points with you once you eat. For two, I've missed the last few family dinners, and this way they won't give me as much shit if I bring a guest."

"Fine. I'll go, but only because I don't feel like cooking anything and now you'll owe me one."

Trying not to let the excitement show on his face, he let the doors close and pressed the button for the garage a few more times before she could change her mind. They were silent the rest of the way, and she followed him to his car, where he opened the passenger door for her.

"Thank you," she said politely and slid into the car, settling her bag between her feet as he closed the door.

Once he was seated in the driver's seat, she began pulling her hair out of its messy bun.

"Were you going to tell me I still had a pencil in my hair before introducing me to your parents?"

He couldn't help but laugh as he started his car and pushed down the bolt of desire from sitting close to her, surrounded by her feminine smell and softness.

"Now that is for sure a trick question. Besides, one of us might have needed it later."

Her usually white-blonde hair hung thick around her shoulders but looked darker in the shadows. The scent of mint and honey filled the space.

"It's your shampoo, that mint scent," he said out loud before realizing how odd that sounded.

"What?"

"You always have this nice, sweet scent of mint, and I couldn't figure out what it was. Sorry, that's weird, but I just got a big whiff when you let your hair down. I like it." He babbled and started to pull the car out of his parking spot. "Just pretend I didn't say that."

She laughed, digging in her bag for something then made short work of pulling her hair back up into a tidy ponytail.

"How come you never wear your hair down?" he asked.

He could feel her eyes on him but kept his on the road. He itched to compliment her, but she likely wasn't ready for him to cross over the professional line that far yet. She didn't answer him. It was starting to drizzle, and the fall weather had put a chill in the air. She retrieved a lightweight army-green coat from her purse and draped it on her lap.

"What else is in your Mary Poppins bag of tricks?"

"Everything I need," she said.

"Everything but a delicious dinner. I should warn you, my father is a retired cop and that combination seems to breed paranoia. He has all sorts of gadgets and unnecessary security measures."

"So he's like a prepper?"

"Sort of. My brothers are also cops, and I apologize for them in advance."

"Why, what will they do?"

"Oh, they'll be perfect gentlemen to you. Their wives are awesome. You'll love them—everyone does. But they will tease and harass and try to embarrass me in front of you. So I'm apologizing for that."

"I feel like you could have led with that earlier, and I would have agreed to go with you sooner."

Lifting his eyebrow, he glanced at the smile on her face. "Oh, okay. So I see you'll be taking their side. Fine. Just remember we have to work together."

"Maybe if you tell me your most embarrassing story now, they can't embarrass you later," she said.

The rain started to fall harder, and he liked the feeling of intimacy it gave them, shuttered away in his smaller coupe, only a few inches apart.

"Nice tactic, but I'm not falling for that one. You'll have to earn your stripes if you want to know my secrets."

"Or ask your brothers. It sounds like they'll be more than happy to fill me in."

He pulled in front of his parents' recently repainted white-and-brick house and parked along the street. The rain was not letting up, so he reached into the back seat for an umbrella. The close quarters of the sporty car forced him into her space, and her breath hitched. Handing her the umbrella, he watched as she pressed her perfectly shaped lips together. It was as if an artist had toiled over drawing the outline of each lip only to entice him to trace them with his finger.

"I'll use my coat. You take the umbrella," she said before popping open her door and stepping out with her coat over her head. Clutching her bag to her chest, she walked quickly along the brick path that led to several steps up to a large front porch.

Sprinting after her with the umbrella, he shook off some of the rain, just as she pushed the hood back off her head, revealing red cheeks. Before he could say anything, a siren wailed, and the sound of a dog barking went off in speakers hidden on the porch. Her body jumped a foot toward him, and he wrapped his arm around her, protectively pulling close. Finally, she seemed to welcome his nearness and pushed closer into his side.

"Shit, my dad's security system. Don't worry—it's all for show."

The door whipped open, and his dad stood with a big grin while holding his puffy white dog, Biff.

"Dad, can we turn off the siren for family dinner?"

"No, son, that would defeat the purpose of having the security system. You should know that." His dad punched in a code in a panel near the door, then opened the storm door for them. "You're late, but since you've brought a guest, you're forgiven."

"Hello, Mr. Maguire. I'm Hailey, and I work with Finn.

I hope you don't mind me intruding on your family dinner."

"Come in, dear. We don't mind at all. Thank you for knocking some sense into our wayward son. He has missed two dinners in a row. On the third offense, we send out a search party." His dad ushered Hailey in and gave Finn a stare down over her head.

"I'm sorry, Dad, really."

"Oh, don't apologize to me. Tell your mother."

Hailey paused and began to remove her coat, but Finn quickly grabbed it and hung it on the wall above a narrow bench. His father moved ahead, but she waited for Finn.

"Don't be nervous. There shouldn't be any more booby traps inside the house," he said. His hand itched to soothe her back again, but he didn't want to overstep her boundaries or make her uncomfortable. "You can leave your bag here if you like." There were several other purses already lined up along the bench.

She set the bag down, and he caught the glimpse of a blue bag inside with what looked like a medical logo.

"Finn, how'd you convince a woman to hang out with you more than once and trick her into a family dinner?"

He hung his head in defeat at the sound of Conner's booming voice.

"Here we go."

To his surprise, a giggle escaped from Hailey.

"I think I made the right decision to join you for dinner," she said and grabbed him by the elbow to lead him toward the interior of the home.

Chapter Five

Hailey

HER PALMS WERE sweating, and her nerves were on end as she bit the inside of her cheek. She wasn't accustomed to sitting at a family dinner, and Finn's family was like some made-for-tv version in the old sitcoms. Everyone was smiling and affectionate, there were cakes and treats on the large kitchen island, but the table was the real event. It was a large white-washed table that could easily seat twelve, adorned with platters of food; pasta, meats, salads, sautéed vegetables, and beautiful place settings. All the while, she had her hand looped through his arm, clutching his ripped bicep like a lifeline, and she couldn't seem to let go.

"This is Sunday dinner?"

Finn shrugged. "Mom's way of keeping tabs on all of us kids—family dinner once a week, required."

Nodding, she braced for the onslaught. Law school and four years working at the firm had taught her how to put on a smile and play the game. She could work a crowd when it was required. Granted, it made her skin crawl and she despised it, but being antisocial and standing in a corner was never going to get her a seat at the partner table, and she didn't have any reason to be intimidated by the people in this house. Finn was warm and professional in every interaction she'd ever had with him.

He'd never hit on her or made her uncomfortable. Until recently, she'd assumed she wasn't his type. Because every other junior lawyer had at some point been unprofessional, and even several of the married clients had been inappropriate and forward.

The couples at the table all stopped talking as they walked farther into the room, and Finn's father stood, clearing his throat. "Ahem. Everyone, Finn has brought a guest. This is Hailey, and they work together at the firm."

In unison, everyone said, "Hello Hailey," and she felt the heat pushing up her neck.

"Hi. I get the feeling Finn doesn't bring a lot of guests to dinner."

One of the men that looked disturbingly like Finn stood. He was taller and leaner, but they were definitely brothers. He stuck out his hand.

"Only because he is a man of discerning taste, and he knows that I will tease him mercilessly when he blows it. I'm Conner, nice to meet you." He turned and smiled wide at a woman with bright orange curly hair. "This is the love of my life, Hannah."

The woman laughed and rolled her eyes. "Hi, Hailey, it's nice to meet you."

"Oh, Finn. You made it." A woman with thick, auburn hair appeared in the hall and moved gracefully to hug him. He lifted her off her feet in a bear hug causing her to laugh.

"Mom, I brought a friend from work. Hailey, this is my

mom, Cora."

"Mrs. Maguire, it's a pleasure to meet you."

"You can call me Cora, dear, and the pleasure is mine. You two are just in time. Have a seat, and we'll get started." She smiled at Hailey before addressing Mr. Maguire. "Put that dog down so we can eat," Cora said.

His mom ushered her to sit in an empty seat next to her, and everyone shuffled a bit so Finn could sit on the other side of Hailey.

"This is my other brother, Rory, and his wife, Ainsley," Finn said.

They both smiled and greeted her warmly. Once his mother said grace, the table was filled with activity. Finn poured her a glass of wine, and she accepted platter after platter of food as they each filled their plates.

"Where are you going to put all of that?" Finn said, looking at the large heaping of pasta and chicken on her plate.

"I may forget a meal here and there, but when I do eat, I make it count."

"I like her already," Conner said. "You're not going to be disappointed. My mom makes the best Marsala ever." After a few bites, she couldn't help but hum at the flavor bomb of garlic, onion, Marsala wine, and butter.

"The key ingredient is butter, lots of butter," Cora said.

"So, Finn, tell us what's been keeping you so busy you had to miss two family dinners in a row," Rory said.

His smile fell, and he looked to his mom before he answered. "Just one of the guys on the team having a tough time lately."

His brother nodded. "Sorry to hear it."

Before anyone asked more questions, he changed the subject. She wondered what he meant by *a tough time*?

"Hailey and I are working this case together. Actually, we're pitted against each other for a shot at the title for junior partner."

Conner made a loud whistle sound. "Damn, just bow out now, dude. They are going to figure out you are prettier than you are smart, and Hailey is going to win."

Everyone laughed, and Hailey startled at the feel of Cora's warm hand on her wrist but was met by a big smile. As a kid, she'd developed a fear of people putting their hands on her, after several bad incidents with foster parents. As an adult, she had to retrain her brain not to always expect the worst out of people. This woman wasn't capable of the kind of pain Hailey had once experienced.

"So you're a lawyer at the firm too then? How exciting. Did Finn tell you I worked there?"

She looked from his mom back to Finn, who looked like a kid caught with his hand in the cookie jar, but also sheepish. She was struck with how handsome he was and the energy between them seemed to spike. "No, he failed to mention he was a legacy." She set her fork down and took a small sip of her wine. "I guess I'm done for now on the partnership."

His mom laughed. "Well, that was a long time ago, and if Baxter Senior has any say, it'll be whoever knows case law backward and forward and has the most intangible but necessary trait in court."

"Which is?" Rory said.

"We used to call it a lot of things: allure, wasta, presence, grace, charisma. A trial lawyer needs to appear to have all of those qualities, all at once. Too cocky, and you're smarmy. Too demure, you're weak. It's a tough balance for many lawyers to come off as both assertive and compassionate in the courtroom."

"Your mom has it. Just do what she does," his dad offered.

"You might have too much of that badassness," Rory teased.

"Hailey has it in the bag. My only hope is if she gets the flu," Finn said.

"We'll see," Hailey said, surprised at how certain Finn sounded that she was the shoo-in for partnership when he had not one but two connections to a senior partner.

"Are you worried about the ole boys club mentality?" Hannah asked from across the table.

"Yes, but I do think Baxter and Stewart are above that fray," Hailey said.

"Hailey is an exceptional lawyer. You should come to our trial just to watch her in action."

Everyone's eyes ping-ponged from Hailey to Finn and back to Hailey.

"The plaintiff has definitely underestimated us, so far," she said to deflect the odd vibe his family was giving off. It was clear they thought there was something more than a professional relationship between them.

The rest of the dinner revolved around embarrassing stories of Finn as a boy, or trouble he and his brothers got into. Their sister, Charlotte, called at one point to say hi to everyone, and they could hear kids yelling in the background. Once everyone was done, Hailey tried to help clear the table, but Finn stopped her.

"Nope, house rules. You can't help clean up. You're my guest."

Handing him her plate, she met his eyes, but the fork slid off her empty plate when her hand started to shake.

"My insulin," she croaked.

Hannah was up on her feet, and Hailey could feel the rush of fog cloud her vision. The room started to go off kilter, and she remembered she had forgotten to take her medicine.

"Hailey, do you have your insulin with you?" Hannah said, crouching at her side.

"She had a blue bag in her purse," Finn said with a twinge of panic in his voice.

She heard his feet hit the floor fast, then he was back by her side, handing her purse to Hannah. Everything looked muted and dark like the night was closing in on things.

"I forgot. That was so stupid," Hailey said as Hannah prepped the thickest part of the back of her bicep.

"It's okay, sweetie. You were having too much fun. You'll be back to normal in a jiff."

"Alright, let's all give her some space," Cora said and ushered everyone away.

Hailey closed her eyes and took a few deep breaths as she waited for the insulin to hit her system. "Your dad is a cop, your mom is a judge, and your sister-in-law is a doctor?"

"Paramedic, but good enough," Hannah teased.

"Is anyone a black sheep in this family?"

"That would be me I guess," Finn said, giving her hand a

squeeze. She hadn't realized, but at some point he'd weaved his strong fingers between hers and gripped her hand. She took a few more breaths before opening her eyes and focusing back on the room, which was empty.

"I guess you know my weakness now," she said, meeting his eyes.

Finn's intense green eyes were a dark shade of jade, and his brow was furrowed. She'd realized at dinner his brothers had the same green eyes, which was clearly from their mom.

"I'm afraid of the dark," he said, in a hushed tone.

"What?"

"My weakness. Now you know mine too."

"You were a Navy SEAL, and you want me to believe you're afraid of the dark."

"Shhhh. Jeez, if my brothers hear this, I'll never ever live it down."

The wooziness finally subsided, and she pulled her hand from his to reach for her water glass. Chugging the cool liquid was the best excuse to break contact and give her a minute to assess what to do next. She never should have agreed to attend dinner with his family. At the same time, she'd never experienced such a warm get-together. And she was interested in speaking to his mom about several cases and her career path to a judgeship.

Finn sat next to her and ran his now-empty hand back and forth over the tablecloth.

"It was on my second mission on the team. We'd swam several miles and discovered our landing point was covered by the fast-moving tide, but the gear we needed to retrieve was in a cavern underwater. We took turns diving and trying to find the opening."

"You must be a very strong swimmer."

"Finally, I found the opening and retrieved the gear, but I'd left my night vision on dry land and dropped the one light I'd had along the slippery rocks. Rookie mistake in every sense."

"Uh-oh."

"I debated whether to find my way back out, but I knew it was a good chance I'd get lost in the tides and run out of oxygen. But if I was the only one who could find the cavern, I might also die before the tide went out again."

His casual smile was gone, and he stared off, as if seeing the dark of the cave all over again.

"But here you are."

He grimaced. "My teammate found me about ten minutes before the cavern filled up, and we swam back to shore."

"Holy crap, you owe him your life."

"We always owe each other our lives on the teams, and any praise we get belongs to our fallen teammates."

"Is that why you don't like talking about it at work? I've heard you deflect every time another lawyer asks you about how hard it was to be a SEAL."

"They don't want to hear a real story," he scoffed. "They want to hear the Hollywood glamorized version."

"I think most people think of our military as heroes."

"I can't speak for every branch in the military, but as for the SEALs, the men that didn't make it out of a mission alive are the only heroes."

"Said like a humble hero. So you're afraid of the dark

because you had to sit in a cave and almost died? That's your weakness?"

He nodded looking around, but everyone had moved outside to chat by a fire pit.

"Do you sleep with a flashlight now, or do you keep every light on in your room?"

The left side of his mouth pulled up. "I do have a night-light and a ton of flashlights in my place. In case the power goes out."

"That's not really something I can use against you."

"I would never use your diabetes against you, Hailey. I'm not going to play dirty to beat you."

She nodded. "May the best lawyer win."

"Agreed," he said, and his hand settled on top of hers, warm and comforting. "You feel up to a cup of tea, or would you rather head home?"

"Tea sounds good. Can we still ask your mom a few questions about that case?"

"Absolutely."

He moved his hand as he stood, and she felt the loss down to her toes. While she took a few deep breaths, he walked into the kitchen to pull down some mugs and turned on the electric teakettle on the counter. She couldn't help but admire the muscular shape of his body visible beneath the dark jeans and a collared dark polo. The muscles of his back showed without any effort on his part, and she would bet the junior partnership that he was ripped along every inch of his tall, confident form. Light auburn hair he kept trimmed into a fashionable business-style cut gave him a boyish look, but it was obvious he was a warrior. It wasn't just that he was older than all the other junior lawyers. Something in his face made it clear he had seen things in life. Just like her but in a totally different way.

He turned abruptly to hold up two kinds of tea and caught her watching him.

"Earl Grey, or cozy night chamomile?"

"I better go with the cozy, or I'll never fall asleep."

He nodded, then poured the steaming water over two cups.

"I'm going to find out who else wants tea, or I'll be back in the doghouse. Just sit tight and relax."

He set the steaming hot cup in front of her and she felt his other hand on the back of her chair, but he didn't touch her. The impulse to reach out to him was strong, but she squashed it down. He was just being a good host and colleague; she shouldn't overthink his kindness for affection. Before she could dwell on it, she heard her name being called from the fire pit. Then he reappeared.

"My brothers would like to question you about how I behave in court, but my mom is coming in so we can talk shop."

She smiled and stood as Cora entered the room, with Hannah and Conner on her heels. They were headed out, but before she left, Hannah gave Hailey a big hug, surprising her with the familiarity.

"Take care of yourself," Hannah said in a concerned tone.

"Thank you for your help. I promise I won't make you work next time I see you," Hailey said, knowing she probably wouldn't see the woman again.

"Alright, you two. Let's sit in the living room, and we can talk," Cora said, grabbing her own tea. "Your father is off on a tangent about training scenarios with Rory, and we'll never get a word in edgewise outside."

For the next hour, they picked Cora's brain about the case Finn remembered and any other cases she knew of that were similar. She was a wealth of knowledge, and Hailey was struck by how measured and intelligent her answers were and how clearly she'd dedicated her life to her family and the law. When it was time to go, Hailey couldn't help but feel disappointed and a little jealous that Finn had grown up with such an advantage. But it wasn't fair for her to project her own sad story on him, even if he was her competition.

His mother packed up enough food to last her the week and made Hailey promise that she would visit her at court whenever she had time.

"No matter what happens with this partner selection, I expect to see you again Hailey, or I'll hunt you down myself," Cora said before she wrapped her in a warm hug.

"Thank you so much for dinner and your wisdom. I promise not to thrash your son in court too badly."

His mom and dad laughed as they walked them to the door. They watched at the threshold as she and Finn walked down the brick path back to his car. It was almost ten o'clock, and the fatigue of the day was hitting her. Finn opened her door, and she reveled in the kind courtesy. It was nice to have someone look out for her for once.

"I think I kept you out too late," he said once he was buckled in next to her.

Resting her head back on the seat, she gazed at him.

"Afraid you'll turn into a pumpkin?"

"No, and I wouldn't need a glass slipper to find you again," he said.

"That would make you Prince Charming. I can see a resemblance." Exhaustion was muddling her mind.

He smiled and pulled the car onto the road. They were both quiet as he maneuvered the twisty streets. The manicured and well-lit sidewalks of his parents' neighborhood turned into old city streets with bus stops and a few homeless people camping on storefronts. In front of her building, he turned off the car and started to get out before she could bother to argue, retrieved the to-go bag his mom packed, and opened her door for her again.

"I'm just going to walk you to the door so I can sleep with a clear conscience."

"It's a perfectly safe neighborhood. Besides, if someone wanted to cause trouble, they would go after the shops where there are more valuables."

"You're valuable, trust me," he said, walking with one hand on her elbow so lightly she didn't realize it was there until he let go.

They stopped in front of the rust-colored steel door that led to the stairwell up to her apartment. She dug for her keys and smiled up at him when she found them.

His forehead was crinkled again.

"What?"

"I just think it would be safer if you lived in a building with a doorman."

"Safer and expensive. I'm fine. I even have this if someone tries to mess with me." She lifted out her Taser to prove she could defend herself.

"And who else has a key to this stairwell?" he asked.

"Only the three other residents. There are four apartments."

He nodded. "I'll walk you to your door."

"Not necessary, Prince Charming. I've lived here for four years, and it's been fine."

She opened the door and accepted the bag of leftovers from him.

"See you tomorrow," he said with a half-smile.

A wave of sadness hit her. Their impromptu night was over, which was absurd because she wasn't going to spend any more time with Finn once this case wrapped up. In fact, if she didn't make partner, she would have to quit the firm. She wasn't going to stay where she wasn't wanted, but more importantly, she couldn't stay at a firm that would use nepotism and the old boys club tactics to select partners. If the partners thought she would just continue to work twice as hard as all the other lawyers for no gain, they were mistaken.

"I can stay if you want, I mean, we can go over the case or whatever," he said.

She realized she was standing in the open doorway but not moving.

"No, it's late. Thanks for dinner. It was really nice to meet your family."

The words were out before she could think, and she did an about-face to stride up the stairs two at a time. She didn't hear the door close, which meant Finn was standing there watching her. Fumbling with the keys, she unlocked her apartment door and scurried inside like a scaredy cat. Her heart raced as she leaned against the inside of her apartment door. She heard the exterior door finally close with a thud. The mellow rumble of his car starting coaxed her to the window, and she found him looking up at her through his windshield. He waved before pulling his car away.

Finn Maguire had gotten into her head and under her skin. He'd been kind and had distracted her. She'd lost sight of her goal tonight and got too comfortable spending time with Finn, wondering if his full lips were soft or firm. But she'd set her sights higher than a hot guy with a nice family. She was going to make partner, and not even Finn's kindness or hypnotizing green eyes were going to stand in her way.

Chapter Six

Finn

MONDAY MORNING, FINN was in a terrible mood after what could only be described as a great night. He liked Hailey, and something about having her by his side at his parents' house felt perfect, like she belonged with him. But he didn't want her to just be his colleague. When she almost fainted and his sister-in-law helped her with her insulin, every instinct to take care of her went into overdrive. Even after she recovered, he'd been tempted to ask her to let him sleep on her couch in case she had another spell, but he knew she'd shoot him down.

Now he needed to figure out how to act normal around her, win their case, and then convince her to let him take her out on a real date. This was new territory for him. Not that he was used to getting any woman he wanted, but it had never been so complicated. He also hadn't ever met someone that compelled him to think about wanting more. Until now, Hailey was someone to admire from afar, but up close and personal, he found her even more beguiling. Holding her hand yesterday, it took every ounce of his power not to pull her into his lap to comfort her. Throughout the evening, he'd caught her watching him with what could only be described as need, and he wanted to give her everything she wanted. He had never wanted more.

As a SEAL, he traveled too much to maintain any kind of a real relationship so he never dated anyone seriously. In law school, he didn't like the distraction or complication of a girlfriend. Since being at the firm, he'd dated a few women, but nothing stuck. No one challenged or intrigued him until Hailey.

"Can you meet in the conference room to go over our case?" The message popped up in a chat box on his computer.

"Ready when you are," he fired back, but the box closed, signaling she'd logged off.

Hailey walked past his office without a word, and he resisted the urge to reach for her. She wasn't looking for a man to chase her. She needed to be wooed, but how was he going to do that and remain professional?

The first step was to win their case. He gathered his notes and laptop before taking the stairs up to their conference room, then grabbed two fresh bottles of water from the well-stocked kitchenette before he popped into the conference room. He may not be able to give her flowers and fancy dinners, but he could be considerate and show up in other little ways to get her attention.

"I didn't find anything yesterday linking the large deposit of cash that started the Pleasure Inc business," Hailey said as soon as he walked in. "We need to look at Mr. Tovar's accounts to see if we can find any links that would prove money was moved from a joint account." She was staring down at several files and had her laptop already open.

"Good morning to you too," he said, causing her head to pop up. Her eyes squinted at him as if to say this wasn't a social hour.

Even her squints were sexy. He was going to have a hard time remaining focused for the next five weeks.

Sitting down, he took a deep breath. They were back to business mode. The relaxed and more open Hailey from the night before was shuttered behind her legal persona.

"Do you think there is anything to find?" he asked.

"No, Mrs. Tovar was clear that she kept everything separate from the start, and it wouldn't have made sense for her to withdraw a large sum then deposit it in her new account and lie about it."

"So we'll scrub the transactions to be safe, and maybe any large withdrawals the year leading up to her business starting. I think we better confirm there is no reference to her husband or Tovar Enterprises on her small-business loan application too," Finn suggested.

She nodded. "Good call."

"I reached out this morning, asking her for any additional family names that could verify the inheritance from her aunt. Apparently, there were only a few living relatives at the time, but she said she would send over the list, which had me thinking."

She stood to walk along the bank of windows while formulating her thoughts. He was gifted the opportunity to watch her long strides in another pantsuit that flowed over her feminine form to accentuate each curve and slope in a way he wasn't sure she intended.

"Correct me if I'm wrong, but Mr. Tovar's attorneys have to prove the money came from a joint account. It's their responsibility to find the evidence to prove their clients' claim. We don't have to prove a negative to win, right?" She stopped to face him.

"That is my interpretation of the law too, but it would be tidier if we had a paper trail to prove our side," Finn said.

Hailey's smile felt like he'd won a marathon.

"Is that how you like things to be, tidy?" she asked.

"When it comes to a case, or my house, otherwise life can be pretty messy," Finn said.

Her smile slipped a bit, but she didn't comment.

"Do you want to handle the scrub on Mr. Tovar's checking account while I do the savings? Then we can swap and double-check each other's work?" she asked, changing the subject.

She stacked several folders in front of her and slid another stack across the conference table toward him.

"Good plan."

"You're good at working on a team. I expected you to try to take over and give orders," she said.

He shrugged, taken back by the compliment. "I guess I had a lot of practice in the military and from planning pranks on my sister."

"I can't imagine that was easy for her, growing up with three brothers."

"Oh, don't underestimate my sister's ability to detect us or my parents' defense of their precious princess," he said with amusement.

A forced smile appeared on her face. "You have a really

amazing family. It must have been idyllic to grow up in that home."

"I take it your experience was very different?"

"Polar opposite." She sat back in her seat and opened the top folder with old receipts and a notebook Mrs. Tovar had identified as her "corporate books" for her first year.

He could take the hint. Her background was a landmine, and he'd have to wait until she was ready to share it with him.

Several hours into spreadsheets, old documents, and paper cuts, Finn wondered if all this was necessary. Or were they looking at this case from the wrong angle?

"Can we take a break and maybe get some lunch? Clear our minds?"

He expected her to say no, but she jumped up and stretched instead.

"I'm so glad you said that. I can't take these accounting slips anymore. I feel like we're wasting time on this."

"I agree. Let's regroup over tacos. I know a place."

"Of course you do, Navy SEAL-turned-foodie lawyer," she teased as they headed for the door.

Not wanting to risk her changing her mind, he pressed the button for the lobby floor in the elevator, but she seemed just as eager to get out of the building for a little bit.

Once outside, Finn paused. "Okay, two years in this office, and I know three things."

"That's it?"

He gave her a warning look but enjoyed the playful smile that pulled at her mouth as he directed her across the street via a crosswalk into a park. He liked that she was loosening up with him again.

"The best coffee is from that stand by the river." He pointed to the edge of the park where a wide path traced the edge of the river. "And the best taco truck is parked on the other end of this park."

"And the third one?" she prompted.

"I better hold out on sharing that one a little longer."

Before responding, she stopped in her tracks. "I forgot to grab my wallet."

"I'll spot you, no big deal. You can buy our next meal."

She hesitated and looked back toward the office.

"Hailey, it's like a five-dollar taco bowl, and I'm going to order the lobster when you're buying."

"Or I'll just pay you back," she said.

"Whatever helps you sleep at night. Now I have an important question. Your taco experience hinges on this."

"Fire away," she said as they proceeded down the sidewalk.

"Do you prefer verde or roja salsa?"

Smiling, she considered the question. "Emm, this is an important decision. I'm going with verde on the taco but roja for the chips."

He clapped his hands as they walked up to the short line. "Excellent, we are officially food compatible."

"Is that important when two people are competing for the same job?"

"Well maybe not, but it makes things easier when two people are working in the trenches together."

He was rewarded with another big smile, but then it was their turn to order. She opted for three street tacos, the same dish he always got, and they agreed to share one bag of chips and salsa. Once their order was up, they sat on a bench that outlined a big concrete fountain, the chips between them.

"I can't believe I've never had these," she said after finishing her first of the three tacos in record time.

"I can."

She wiped her mouth, then sipped her drink.

"Is that judgment I hear?"

"No, I just mean you're too driven at work. Focused. That's commendable. You also don't walk through this park on your way to court or, I'm guessing, on your route home."

She studied him. "It sounds like you've been paying more attention than I realized."

He wanted to flirt with her, and tell her of course he'd been noticing her, but he wasn't sure if that would go over well.

"Just old habits to pay attention to my surroundings. Like I've noticed one of the senior partners disappears at lunchtime for hours, and several of the newest rookies come in smelling like breweries every Monday morning."

"Kids today," she teased after scarfing down another taco.

"What do you think is Tovar's real angle? Does he want to just bully his soon-to-be ex-wife into giving him her company out of spite? Or is it more?" he asked, changing the subject. She didn't need to know that he'd been admiring her with curiosity since he started with the firm.

Hailey nodded. "I don't like to take my client's word for it, but I think Mr. Tovar is a dirtbag, and Mrs. Tovar is telling the truth about her company. Mr. Tovar has had three sexual complaints filed against him, according to the chatty woman in HR at Tovar Enterprises. A few years ago, the board voted him out of a leadership role, and he's nothing more than a figurehead, spending most days at his club in Arlington."

"Did you do recon without me?" He was impressed with what she'd managed to dig up so far.

"I like to cover my bases and made a few calls. What do you think?"

"I don't think they have any proof to support his claim that he funded her company. I think he's self-righteous and entitled."

"But if we aren't prepared to defend it, we could look foolish in court. We can't get complacent," she said.

"Complacency breeds failure. I'm familiar with that old gem," Finn said, reaching for a chip, and his hand collided with hers. Instead of pulling away, she stole the chip he reached for and ate it.

"What's the toughest part of being a SEAL?" she asked.

He was surprised at her personal question. Until now, she hadn't asked him anything about himself.

"The hardest part was leaving for a mission and not knowing if I'd return."

Their eyes held each other's, and something raw passed over her face. Like she'd felt the same fear and emptiness before. He wondered if she had nightmares too, or managed to chase her bad memories away with pure willpower. For months after his last mission, he'd struggled to get a good night's sleep without medication. Even now, if he didn't exhaust his body with a workout before bed, he'd have a restless night's sleep with memories of missions that had been tough or gone wrong.

"We should get back," she said, breaking through his thoughts.

Both their baskets were empty.

"But what about a dessert?" he said, trying to lighten the moment.

"Really? Do you have a treat after every meal?"

"Now who is judging?" Standing, he grabbed their trash and tossed it out. "Besides, it's on our way back, sort of."

She shook her head but fell into step with him. They were both quiet until they exited the park, and he pointed to a cookie shop across the street.

"I better not, but you go ahead," she said.

He flinched. Only an idiot offered cookies to a diabetic.

"I'm sorry. We can skip it."

"No way. I wouldn't want to deal with a cranky man child who missed his dessert the rest of the day."

On instinct, he reached out to touch her, just a gentle tickle on her side, but she reared back and almost fell off the curb. He was forced to pull her closer to him, and in the next second, their bodies were flush against each other. Her arms tensed for a moment, but then she melted into his arms, each part of her melded to him like a missing half.

"I didn't know you were so ticklish or responsive."

Her eyes were like deep blue pools with unknown depths he wanted to dive into. Her chest heaved, her lips parted, and her eyes fell to his mouth. She relaxed further, pressing into him with no resistance. He was only a few breaths away from kissing her when she came to her senses.

"My sides are very ticklish, and I expect you not to take advantage of that, now that you know."

"I'll try to warn you next time I'm going to tickle you."

Her face lit up with mischief, and her hands settled on the front of his chest over his suit blazer.

"Something tells me that won't help me avoid it."

He let his hands drop as she stepped away and instantly missed how she'd felt in his arms the second she was gone.

"Maybe I'll have shaved ice," she said, reading the neon sign from across the street in the cookie shop window.

Clearing his throat, he reminded himself not to push his luck.

"They're good. I'll get one too—something to cool us down." His voice was strained, but she didn't comment.

They each tried the coffee-flavored shaved ice as they walked back to the office, and he knew he wanted to spend more time with her outside of work. As expected, her demeanor changed the closer they got to the office until the casual version of Hailey was replaced by his colleague and competitor. But he was going to figure out more ways to spend time with her because there was no doubt in his mind she was the real prize in this competition for partner.

Chapter Seven

Hailey

AFTER LUNCH AND several more hours of sifting through financial documents, they decided to file their own request for financial disclosure of Mr. Tovar's personal financial portfolio. Multiple accounts weren't included in the initial tranche of discovery shared with them, and they needed to know why. When they returned from the courthouse, Hailey noticed a buzz in the rookie bullpen. Before she made it to her desk, another one of the rookie lawyers blocked her path. Smith was an Ivy League graduate and walked around like an entitled punk that was better than all the other rookies. He was always making snide remarks about the junior associates that went to state colleges, like Hailey.

"Looks like Maguire won that bet: he managed to thaw the ice queen," Smith said with a tone of distaste. "Pay up, fellas."

"You should've learned in that online law school that it's illegal to gamble at work," Finn said.

"As if, Maguire. You know I went to Yale."

"I don't know. I've never actually seen your degree, and

you lost your last two cases. Not sure they would claim you," Finn replied.

Hailey moved past both of them to her office at the end of the rookie hallway. Some days she wondered if dealing with all the pretentious power plays was even worth it. But the truth was, people like Smith existed at any firm. She was used to people judging her for her education, her looks, and sex. She understood people like Smith drew power by cutting others down or trying to make people feel small. She'd met every kind of bully and had suffered enough real abuse to know he was just getting revved up, and she didn't want any part of it. But she'd get the last laugh when she made partner and took over managing the rookies. No more snobby slackers.

The junior associates dispersed after Finn called out Smith's lack of performance on his cases, and Finn didn't bother to check on her. He knew to leave her alone, or he was hoping she'd forget that Smith implied he was involved in some bet about her.

Once she logged into her company email, a note from Finn popped up in the instant messenger app.

For the record, I didn't participate in any bets.

Ok, Counselor, she fired back.

Permission to approach the bench. We need to discuss the next steps if our hunch on the financials is wrong.

I'll meet you in the conference room in a few hours. I just need to pay some attention to my other cases, Hailey responded.

Deal.

Two hours later, after scouring through financial law code in several large volumes of federal business law codes, she realized she forgot to meet Finn downstairs in the conference room. She always found it easier to read a real book than an e-document, but they were cumbersome. Gathering her notes and the books, she entered the large wood-paneled elevator. The doors closed and she began to descend, but the elevator stopped on the partner floor first. When the doors opened, she was faced with Mr. Baxter, Finn, and another man she didn't recognize. She gave the man a passing glance and fixed her stare on Finn as she moved to the back of the elevator, and they each walked in. Hopefully, it was burning a hole through his immaculate suit and tie to his deceptive heart.

While she was off researching their case, he was schmoozing with Mr. Baxter. She should have known she wasn't the only person he'd be using his Maguire charm on.

"Hailey, you spend so much time in that library, we should move your desk in there," Mr. Baxter said, turning back to face her and smiling.

"Not a bad upgrade as a reward for a junior partner," she fired back.

Mr. Baxter laughed. "Finn, I almost feel like we sent you into battle unarmed."

"I have a few moves left, sir," Finn said, meeting her stare head-on. "Although, I'll admit working with Hailey has forced me to dig deep and get creative."

The elevator dinged on the fourth floor where she planned to meet Finn in their conference room. Moving past the men, she made a point to roll her eyes at Finn so he knew she was onto his tricks.

"Good day, gentlemen," she said as she exited. She heard Finn say goodbye to the men also, but she kept moving toward their conference room at the end of the hall.

"Hey, where's the fire? I can help you with those books if you slow down," Finn said as his smooth stride outpaced her and he opened the door for her.

Once inside, she turned so fast he almost ran into her. The books in her arms shifted, and he put his hands over hers to take over the load. His strength was undeniable, but her body's reaction was immediate attraction. It was annoying, to say the least.

"Is meeting with Baxter privately part of your campaign to win? Sucking up to the senior partner is kind of cliché, don't you think?"

She was being hard on him, but she couldn't win a competition in charming the partners. She relied on hard work to impress people.

"Did you just admit you find me charming?" Finn asked.

His hands still covered hers as he pulled the books from her grasp. A smile spread on his face.

"Move to strike. You don't have to answer that."

She let out a breath. Whew, she didn't need to perjure herself.

"Mr. Baxter was meeting with Admiral Maddox and was gracious enough to introduce me at the end of his meeting. Maddox is a former SEAL too."

"I guess that's an aspect of your experience I can't compete with."

"I actually think this joint case is more about conquering our own weaknesses and how we work together, not our previous accomplishments."

"Then I'm at even more of a disadvantage because you

grew up in a tight-knit family, where I'm guessing you were forced to work together, and then you served on an elite team where you established physical and mental toughness. I'm used to working solo. Trusting our teamwork to result in me winning the partnership is a big fall."

Finn gave up trying to help her with the books and rested his hands on his hips as he pinned her with his eyes.

"Yes, I can work well with others, and I'm mentally and physically strong, but so are you. I suspect we've both had to fight for our lives in different ways—only I had weapons." He took a step toward her. "You're a true survivor, and a brilliant lawyer."

"You really think so?" she asked in a moment of self-conscious weakness.

"Without a doubt," he said with no hesitation.

His eyes were disarming, and the butterflies in her stomach were like a herd of elephants. A shiver ran up her arms, and her cheeks heated. The intensity of his eyes forced her to accept he wasn't playing a game. Or if he was, he was a master and she was losing.

A smile spread on his face. "Now, Little Miss Sunshine, what did you discover in these books while I was glad-handing?"

Taking a deep breath, she set the load on the table and whisked off her blazer. Her body was hot, and her hands were clammy.

"Okay, I did find something, I think." Picking up the largest book, she popped it into the crook of her arm and then realized the irreparable error she made.

She'd forgotten today, of all days, she had worn a short

sleeve blouse under her blazer—a top that exposed a jagged scar along the inside of her bicep. An injury inflicted on purpose by a foster parent that had no business taking care of kids. She had several other old mementos left on her skin from her years dealing with other foster care kids, rough schools, and adults that used physical punishments to gain control. These scars were ugly and one of her most guarded secrets. She found Finn's eyes on her. He stood with his arms hanging stiff at his sides, fists clenched, and his jaw locked tight.

She knew the shape and lines of the ugly scar made it abundantly clear she'd been burned.

"Do not pity me. I'm fine." She set down the book and picked up her blazer to put it back on.

"I won't pity you if you stop hiding from me. You don't have to tell me what happened, but you don't need to be so guarded. I won't judge you or screw you over," Finn said with a calm tone she couldn't help but believe. "You don't need to cover them either. It's nothing to be ashamed of."

"You should use that tone in court. You could convince anyone of anything."

"I mean it, Hailey, but just promise me you're safe now."

"It all happened when I was a kid. I'm as safe as you, minus your warrior skills."

He nodded and then pulled out his military-issue glasses, and she couldn't resist the humor that bubbled up when this tough, ripped, former SEAL put on dorky, thick black plastic glasses.

"Did you just laugh at me?" he asked with a grin.

"No, I would never. It's just that those glasses are so

unique." She reached up and adjusted the frames that did nothing to disguise his handsome face.

"Someone broke mine last week. You'll have to try to resist me with these chick magnets on."

Another bout of laughter struck her, but if she had to guess, most women wouldn't turn him away even with those glasses on. Instead of insanely hot, with the quirky glasses, he looked playful but still gorgeous.

"I'll do my best," she said, trying to ignore the desire rising up her body in the form of another blush.

By seven p.m., they'd found a case law that supported a spouse's use of joint funds to start a private, individually owned company. Moreover, if it was incorporated, it was protected from joint distribution in divorce. Before she could suggest they order dinner, Finn looked at his watch, and the side of his mouth scrunched up. It was his subtle tell that meant he needed to be somewhere else. She'd learned to pick up on a person's body language at a young age. It told her when someone was going to yell, lash out, and when she should run.

"Hot date tonight?" The words slipped out before she could think twice.

"Not a date, more like an appointment. Do you mind if we call it a night? I can work later tomorrow."

"Sure."

Finn paused and studied her.

"Actually, why don't you come with me?"

Before he could explain the invitation, she responded with her standard response when any man at work asked her out.

"No, thanks. I have plans too."

His movements stilled, and he didn't speak until she met his gaze.

The look of disbelief on his face almost made her cave.

"I'm meeting with a group of former teammates. It's casual."

"I've never been to war, Finn."

"I have a feeling that's not exactly true. But it's more of a celebration. It's the Navy's birthday, and the SEALs in the area get together with friends. There will be other civilians."

"That's nice." Her heart pounded at the idea of going anywhere with him outside of work, and the idea of being his friend. That sounded like trying to work in an ice cream shop and never having a single scoop.

Standing, he gathered his notes from the table.

"We'll be at the Limerick Bar, if you change your mind. They have amazing pot pies and tasty local IPA beer. In case you need more of an incentive."

Laughing to herself, she tried to rid her mind of the idea of him as her dessert.

"Okay, thanks for the invite, but I probably won't see you there."

His playful smile lit up with an intensity she hadn't seen before.

"Are you laughing at me?" she asked. Could he somehow read her unprofessional thoughts about him?

"No. More like laughing at myself. You've successfully and firmly made it clear you don't want to be friends. But it just makes me want to try harder."

Her mouth fell open, and her mind turned to mush. The

overpowering urge to kiss the smile off his handsome face made her stand too.

"You want to be my friend?" In that moment, she would have guessed there was a different, more physical reason he'd invited her to the bar.

"For starters, yes. You're interesting, a puzzle, witty and funny when you let your guard down a little. Also we both enjoy good food and mint, so it makes sense that we'd be friends. In my mind."

"Mint?"

He leaned closer. "Your hair smells like a sugary mint."

His dashing smile pulled up more on the left side, leaving his lush lips in a pout. He was sexy and adorable all at the same time. It wasn't fair how disarming he was.

"I don't usually have time for friends, and people at work will assume it's something else between us."

"Maybe you need to make time for friendships, and it doesn't really matter what the other rookies think. You'll be their new boss in no time."

The implication was that he thought she would win the junior partnership. Before she could respond, he pushed in his chair and made a move toward the door.

"See you later if you change your mind, or tomorrow," he called and then was gone.

Hailey stewed for another twenty minutes. Her personal life was a little sad with only a few people she would consider friends. Maybe it wouldn't be so bad if she tried to be friends with Finn. He already knew two of her secrets. But it didn't mean they had to hang out together outside of work. She'd planned to go to her gym tonight anyway.

After locking up the conference room, she changed into her sweatpants in the lobby ladies' room before leaving for the night. She took a local bus to the jiu jitsu gym where she practiced self-defense techniques.

In college, they offered free classes to students, and she'd been studying the skills since. Her childhood was spent worrying about what to do if someone tried to hurt her, and jiu jitsu class was the first time she felt confident about defending herself. She'd barely escaped her last foster care home and had the scars to prove it. Finn had seen one of the remnants of a not great childhood, but there were others, and some no one could see. The burn was the last time anyone put their hands on her and the catalyst that forced her to run away at sixteen.

She'd been terrified someone would find her, but it turned out, no one bothered. As a foster kid, she'd been desperate to find some kind of family and started bugging her social worker about her history. Eventually, the overworked case manager let her read her file. With just a few names listed in her bio, she managed to track down her maternal grandmother in Virginia Beach. Arriving on the stranger's doorstep after several days of bus rides, she easily convinced her only living relative to let her stay until she turned eighteen. The older woman was living on Social Security, a recovered alcoholic, and happy to have someone help her around the house. Hailey made herself as useful as possible, got her GED, and enrolled in the local community college. Then she attended the local state college while working two jobs, graduated with honors and met a professor who said she had a mind for law.

Walking through the well-lit gym, she shook off the memories of her past. A slight man with jet-black hair trimmed in a crew cut style greeted her. He was the manager and owner of the gym.

"What's happening, Hay?"

"Ready to tussle?" she replied.

"Yes, always. I'm glad you made it. We have a few new women joining the class this evening."

Although Hailey didn't like people very much, she did enjoy helping women learn self-defense. It was a crucial survival skill, one she wished she'd had sooner in life. She visited the gym at least two nights a week. One night, she trained with one of the instructors, and the other night, she helped the instructor out by acting as a subject for new students to see techniques they could learn to master.

An hour later, she chugged her water and wondered if Finn was looking for her at the bar. Throughout the entire class, she was distracted by his flirty green eyes that kept popping into her mind. He'd gotten under her skin with his friendship comment, and she had to admit she was curious about him.

After cooling down, she decided to go for one beer and prove to him she wasn't a complete loner. Maybe to prove to herself that she wasn't antisocial, just selective about the company she kept.

Chapter Eight

Hailey

WALKING INTO THE crowded Irish pub, she started to feel nervous that she'd played herself. Finn's group wasn't easy to spot because every man in the bar looked like a current or former Navy SEAL. There were plenty of women in the bar too, but the testosterone was high.

"Hello there, young lady. Are you looking for someone in particular?" a large man in scrubs, with a beard and a scar over his right eye asked with a friendly smile. He was carrying four beers in his massive hands. Her hesitation must have shown on her face, because he smiled bigger.

"Finn Maguire," she said, doubtful he'd know where in the crowd Finn would be. But his face lit up more, if that was possible.

"Follow me, he's back here." He moved forward, "make a hole," he bellowed, and people did.

She followed, unsure it was the smart thing to do but recognized the SEAL trident tattooed along his forearm and decided to have some faith. A rare occurrence for her. A path spread like Moses parting the Red Sea but quickly closed behind her.

Suddenly, he stopped short.

"Maguire, I found someone of yours," the large man said as he set down the beers on the high-top table at the rear of the pub.

Warmth spread up her chest at the thought of belonging to Finn. Clearing her throat, she stepped to the side of the large man and found several clean-cut men who all looked like fitness models staring back at her. Finn was talking to someone on the other side of the table, but his eyes sparkled and his kissable lips spread in a huge smile when he spotted her.

"You changed your mind," Finn said, leaning over the table to pluck up one of the fresh beers and hand it to her. "Beer?" he asked, but she heard several of the other men grumble.

"Gentlemen, respect Finn's ability to elevate our sophistication with a lady's presence, please," the large man with the beard said and winked at her.

Accepting the beer, Hailey took a sip of the cold IPA and was at a loss on what to say.

"Guys, this is my friend Hailey. These are the guys," Finn said, still grinning ear to ear.

There was a round of hellos while Finn muscled his way through the others around the table to stand next to her.

"You're just in time," he said close to her ear.

"For what?" she asked just as someone rang a large brass bell hanging over the bar seven times.

The crowded bar grew completely quiet, and the music stopped.

The bartender read off several names, then everyone held

up their glasses and in unison said, "to the brotherhood," before taking a long sip from their drinks. She followed Finn's lead.

"Those are the names of SEALs who died this year," Finn explained.

"Only five," she whispered. "I mean, that's horrible, but your profession seems inherently dangerous."

"Every hour, they read several names," he said.

"Oh."

"So, Hailey, how'd a nice girl like you get tangled up with Maguire?" the bearded man asked.

"Who said I was nice?" she fired back.

The men listening laughed, and embarrassment from the implication of her words made her want to unzip her lightweight but long-sleeve sweatshirt. The bar was packed, so it was already warm, and standing so close to Finn with his friends' eyes on her left her feeling the heat.

"Fair point. Then I have to ask, are you hoping to corrupt our golden boy? Because I'll warn you it's impossible. I've tried," the bearded man said.

Finn grimaced and took another sip of his beer.

"You mean he's even more perfect than I thought? Not one flaw?"

"Not a single tarnish, but if you're more interested in bad boys, I could use a new friend," another guy with deep dimples and a bald head said. He'd been standing at the table since she'd arrived, quietly listening.

"Easy, Cozmo, Hailey's off-limits. Go flirt with someone else," Finn said with more bite than she would have expected from him with his friends.

Cozmo held up his hands. "Okay, bro. I get it. But you can't blame me."

Hailey sipped her beer. Did Finn not want his friends to flirt with her because they were colleagues or because he considered her his to flirt with?

"Sorry. If you don't have a ring, it's fair to say any man in this bar will think you're available," Finn said.

"It's okay. I guess technically, I am." She set down her beer and shrugged out of her sweatshirt, unable to take the warmth any longer. Her fitness T-shirt was simple black but snug in the shoulder area and had high sleeves.

"So you were telling me something about the golden boy," she prompted the man Finn referred to as Dalton.

The large man sat half perched on a stool but was still at least a foot taller than her. Broad shoulders and the coiled muscles of his forearms indicated his dedication to his strength, but there was an underlying sophistication to him.

He held out his hand. "Where are my manners? If I'm going to spill all the tea about our golden boy, we should be properly introduced. Dalton Hart—you can call me Hart."

She shook his large hand and could tell he was being gentle with her much smaller one, but if he wanted, he could crush her like a bug.

"Thank you for the beer," she said.

"Finn here was top of our BUD/S training class and annoyingly good at everything. I myself was a Division One-level athlete and not used to being beat by anyone when we met. As you can imagine, it took Finn and me some time to develop a friendship. He became the bar by which we all compared ourselves and the rabbit we all attempted to beat."

"Doesn't the rabbit die in that scenario?" she asked, glancing from Finn's serious face to Dalton's broad smile.

"Well, technically, but we just wanted to beat him at something. I don't think anyone would have hurt him." Dalton eyed Cozmo, whose face seemed more serious.

"Nah, not permanently anyway," Cozmo said.

"Before we tell you something you already know, what dirt do you know about our golden boy?" Dalton asked.

She took another look at Finn, not expecting his emerald-green eyes to be gleaming back at her with something she couldn't name. Was it interest in what she knew about him or concern over what she might say?

"Well, he's a team player, never complains, never objectifies the women in the office, always opens doors for me, loves his mother, respects his father, and..." She paused.

"And," Dalton prompted.

"And he likes to fight for the underdog. I even spotted him helping an old lady across the street last week."

The group groaned.

"How can you stand it?" Dalton said.

"Everyone needs at least one person to balance out their bad," she offered.

Dalton looked her over. "No offense, deary, but you don't strike me as bad. No tattoos, no crazy piercings I can see." His eyebrow wiggled, and her cheeks began to ache from smiling. "Do you have some brass knuckles in your pocket?"

"No, nothing like that, but I'm not golden, that's for sure." She took another long sip of her beer and then fiddled with the glass.

"Hailey is another junior attorney at our firm. She's my competition for partner and she's brilliant," Finn added.

"Well then you're screwed, Maguire, but you don't really want to be stuck making eight figures at some private law firm anyway," Dalton said.

Hailey was surprised to hear that, since Finn had worked for several years at the firm already. The next step was to seek a junior partnership.

Finn caught the question that hung in the air.

"They like to try to convince me to rejoin the team," he explained.

"Would you?" she asked. Her heart dropped. The idea of him being in harm's way bothered her, but she wasn't ready to admit that to anyone.

"No, barring a World War III scenario, the team doesn't need me. I'm happy with my decision to retire my trident, but I do miss it sometimes."

Feeling eyes on her, Hailey found Cozmo checking out the scar on her bicep when he returned to their table with more beers.

"Hey, bad girl, I got one of those." He pulled up his sleeve to show a gash in his lower shoulder. "From a bayonet in Afghanistan, an old ass weapon but still very effective."

She cringed. Then Dalton pulled up the side of his shirt to reveal a burn on his side the size of her hand.

"Mortar shrapnel."

"You don't have to compare injuries with these idiots," Finn said.

"What about you? Did you ever get hurt on duty, golden boy?" she asked.

Suddenly, she needed to know if he'd ever experienced the searing physical pain that followed when your flesh was stabbed or burned, and the painful elements of recovery. Besides their law degrees, did they have anything else in common?

Up until recently she'd put Finn in the same category as all the other rookie lawyers with fancy degrees and family pedigrees. Granted, he'd served his country and on arguably one of the most elite military teams, but they were still from different backgrounds. But there was something about knowing someone had lived through the kind of hurt and pain that resulted in scars like the ones she had. It made her feel less alone. She was struggling to keep Finn at arm's length, and she wasn't sure she wanted to.

Finn took a long pull of his beer before answering. His eyes held a challenge.

"I was shot three times in the leg in Syria. There was no field hospital in sight. Dalton patched me up, and we had to wait a day for our rescue before I was flown to Germany. But I'm not dropping my pants in the bar to show you."

"So golden of you, Maguire. Once again," Cozmo complained. "You get an invitation by a beautiful woman to drop your pants, and you're too bashful to take advantage of it."

Laughing, Hailey picked up her beer and took a sip. She never spoke about what caused her scars, but they had all so easily offered up what she was sure were dangerous and violent incidents that left them with scars. It might be nice to be open and honest. She could tell they weren't going to think any less of her for it. It was like a camaraderie she didn't know she needed, but maybe Finn had guessed and that was why he invited her tonight?

She held up her arm to show the long gash along her bicep. “Fireplace poker the first time he stabbed me with it. Then he heated it up to singe the wound closed. He didn’t want to have to explain to the social worker what happened if he took me to the hospital.” She ran a hand over the gnarled skin.

Finn’s jaw flexed, but Dalton spoke first.

“You just give us a name, no questions asked.”

And she believed him, but she shrugged it off.

“He’s dead. The next kid he tried to mess with had already had enough scars and fought back,” Hailey said.

“So it does make sense that you and Finn would get along. Two survivors of war,” Cozmo said, breaking the silence. “He ever tell you about the time he got stuck in a cave?”

“Were you the one who found him?” she asked.

Cozmo’s eyebrows lifted dramatically before he looked to Finn, and something passed between them.

“Yes, he’s lucky I’m half fish,” Cozmo finally said.

Her stomach grumbled, and she checked her watch; if she didn’t have something soon, her insulin would drop. As if he could read her mind, Finn piped up.

“You wanna get a bite to eat before these guys really embarrass me?” His hand moved to gently settle on the small of her back right before a group of women accidentally bumped into her.

His touch steadied her, but her body was pressed against his, and the feel of his warmth and muscular strength sent shivers of desire over her.

"I think I actually better call it a night." She set down the unfinished beer and grabbed her sweatshirt. "It was nice to meet you all. If you ever need a lawyer, look me up."

The guys all said good night, and Finn followed her out the door. On the street, they were met by the quiet of late evening and a cool breeze.

"I'm glad you came tonight," he said.

She pulled on her sweatshirt quickly and battled the urge to smile at him.

"Me too. Your friends are interesting. It's nice you've all been through so much together and kept in touch."

He nodded, but the look in his eyes was different from his usual confidence. He seemed unsure of what to say or do next. She was captivated by it, holding her breath to see what he would decide.

"Can we pretend for the next hour we're not colleagues or just friends? Let's be Hailey and Finn spending time together because we want to figure out what this is between us."

She gulped. "Okay." Her response was out before she could overthink it.

His serious face broke into a proud grin.

"Great. Come on, I know a place I think you'll love." His hand settled on the small of her back to guide her toward a crosswalk. Then he wove his fingers with hers to hold her hand. Downtown Alexandria was filled with old cobblestone streets, row homes with colorful flowers on their brick stoops, and several blocks of shops and restaurants. They were both quiet as Finn guided her to a blue awning a block away. There was a bright neon dumpling moving in the window.

"Dumplings?"

"Only the best dumplings I've ever had in the States." He opened the door for her.

She couldn't help but think they were crossing a serious threshold, an imaginary line where nothing had to keep them apart. As colleagues, she knew it was a bad idea to get involved. As competitors for the same promotion, it was idiotic. But those were rules she created to stay focused and avoid being viewed as anything other than a serious and dedicated attorney. Now she was setting all of that aside to spend time with a man that made her heart pound, skin tingle, and she couldn't stop thinking about. In that moment, she had to admit to herself that she wanted to be closer to Finn, in every sense of the word.

A hostess ushered them to a booth with red bench seats. Hailey was surprised Finn chose to sit on the same side with her, as if he knew she wanted his nearness. His thigh pressed against hers, and her arm rubbed against his. But the strangest thing was, her instinct wasn't to create space between them. If anything, she craved to be physically closer to him.

Finn opened the menu on the lacquered wooden table and set it between them.

"Are there any allergies or aversions I need to know about?"

"No."

The energy between them was palpable.

"Do you want to look at the menu, or should I just order what I know is good?" he asked.

"Why don't you just order? I like the idea of not having

to make any decisions."

"Done."

The waitress arrived with water and took the order from Finn, and then they were alone again. He leaned back along the cushioned bench with his hands on the edge of their table. But his head was turned toward her, and she met his stormy eyes.

"Hailey, I'm extremely attracted to you," he said, not breaking eye contact but pausing to give her time to digest what he'd said. "But I'm also crystal clear that you don't date people you work with. I was just hoping you might consider making an exception. I think you must feel this connection between us, or you wouldn't be here right now."

With more bravery than she knew she had, she laced her fingers over his. He moved their locked hands below the table to rest on her thigh, her slender hand safe in his strong one.

Tracing the lines of their intertwined fingers with her other hand, she took a deep breath.

"I'm open to suspending reality tonight," she whispered before meeting his searching eyes.

His free hand moved up to cup her chin, and she turned her cheek into his touch on instinct.

"I want to kiss you, but I don't want to push my luck."

"You won't," she whispered.

He closed the space between them. His full, firm lips pressed hers gently as his thumb ran over her cheek. A kaleidoscope of sensations flowed through her. Pleasure, need, excitement, and fear of the unknown bounced around in her mind, now muddled with the yearning Finn was unraveling inside her. His lips were gentle and coaxing, but an urgent wish to feel more of him rose inside her. She opened her mouth to taste him and was rewarded with the pressure of his tongue against hers. His hand caressed her with care, like she was a piece of glass that might break in his hands.

The sound of several dishes being placed on the table broke through their bubble. She could feel him smile with his lips still pressed to hers, and it was the most intimate and sweetest moment she'd ever experienced. He pulled back, and his eyes twinkled like green gems.

"Let's eat fast so we don't squander our hour," he said.

Hailey avoided the server's eyes. She knew her cheeks were several shades of red.

"I probably won't turn into a pumpkin until midnight, so I think we have some time."

"Then the night is young," he said.

There was a large metal bowl filled with sautéed vegetables and meat, balanced over a flame, steam baskets filled with dumplings, several sauces in small white bowls, and a large container of rice. But the hunger she felt wasn't just for nourishment. Finn was invading her solitary life, and she liked it.

"Where do we start?" she asked.

"You might need one of your hands," he said, giving her fingers still in his lap a squeeze. She'd had both her hands wrapped around his one strong manly hand.

Her cooling cheeks heated again. This man made her blush about eighty percent of the time she was with him. Letting go of his hand was a loss she didn't want to admit.

Then his hand fell to her thigh and settled there.

"Lucky for me, I'm a lefty," he said.

Smiling, she reached for a pair of chopsticks and tried to calm her pounding heart. Had she just made out with a colleague in a restaurant? What had come over her? Their kissing would change everything, and they couldn't pretend it didn't happen.

"You're freaking out, aren't you?" He added a few dumplings to his plate.

"No, not freaking out exactly," she lied.

"Well, I'll admit I am. I didn't think you'd agree to let down your guard this much with me, much less let me kiss you. And now that I know this spark between us is mutual and ready to combust, I'm going to need more than an hour or two with you."

His eyes were on her, and she struggled to meet them, knowing he'd see the passion his words were creating inside her.

"I want to know the real Hailey, the relaxed version I've caught glimpses of. You in your natural state with no boundaries or pretenses, like we didn't meet at work, and we're not competing for anything more than each other's attention."

His hand grazed her chin, lifting it up until she met his eyes. Like two green tractor beams, he was pulling her into his idyllic world, where she could let him shower her with all the emotion vibrating between them. But what if it left her feeling more empty and alone than she already was? She didn't have relationships based on emotions. She wasn't sure she even knew how to care for someone properly, much less receive it in return.

"I'm attracted to you too, Finn, but the circumstances are complicated."

"It's not just the physical desire between us. There's something else here. I know you don't need me to look after you or treasure you, but that doesn't mean I don't want to. You're all I can think about anymore. Even this case has only become a means to be close to you."

Her heart pounded. No one had ever made her feel so wanted or special in her entire life. How could a man she barely knew have such power over her in such a short period of time? Was it even possible it was real? Fiddling with her chopsticks, she considered what to say. For the first time in her life, she wasn't worried about what someone wanted from her, Finn was genuine and honorable. The powerful connection between them was undeniable now. She had wanted the junior partnership for so long, but the even bigger issue was, she wanted Finn now too, emotionally and physically. Even if it wasn't going to last, she couldn't find the will to resist him.

"We would have to agree to some ground rules," she said. "At work we're only professional colleagues, competing for the same promotion. No flirting, no touching, we maintain professional distance at all times."

"I can do that. I mean, the last thing I want is the partners knowing I'm whipped or the junior associates to think I'll be your pet when you win. I'm more than a pretty face and don't plan on being a kept man at work." His mouth was spread in a playful, boyish smile.

Her face ached from smiling, and she impulsively leaned

over to kiss him.

"We need to take this slow so I don't have a panic attack," she said.

"Whatever you say. Just let me kiss you after hours and on weekends."

He leaned forward and kissed her again as his hand gripped her thigh. When he pulled away, they were both breathing heavily.

"What a strange night," she said.

"Don't overthink it. Let's just let ourselves be together."

"Okay."

Picking up the cooled dumpling with her chopsticks, she dipped it in the brownish-red sauce.

"Careful—that one has a bite to it, followed by a lot of heat."

"Hmmm, sounds like exactly what I need."

She took a big bite and let herself enjoy the moment with Finn's eyes on her, desire rolling off him.

Maybe she needed something more than what she'd spent years working for.

Maybe she did need a man to cherish her, but it couldn't be at the expense of her goal for professional security. She needed to keep her eyes on the prize. As partner in the firm, she would have a guaranteed eight-figure salary, student loans paid off, a pension, and autonomy. She was one case away from making junior partner, and not even the delicious desire Finn stirred could dissuade her. But if he thought he could compartmentalize their personal and work relationships, who was she to argue?

Chapter Nine

Finn

THE NEXT MORNING, Finn couldn't be sure if he'd dreamed about kissing Hailey, or if it was real. He was eager to get to the office and see her, but then remembered his promise. He would be completely professional, no behavior that could lead anyone to believe that they were anything more than competitors.

No one would know they'd closed the dumpling restaurant down then made out in his car like two high school students afraid to take things further. When it was clear kissing wasn't going to be enough, he walked her to the door and made sure she got into her apartment safely before he went home and took a cold shower. She'd been careful not to share any personal details about growing up, but he did find out she'd never had a passport, loved to watch black-and-white movies, and collected obscure books after finding a rare first edition at a yard sale.

She was an enigma and he wanted to learn everything about her, but it was clear he would have to treat her like an IED, with a hairpin trigger ready to explode. But her walls were falling fast, once she determined she could trust him.

Now wasn't the time to slow down. She'd agreed to see him outside of work, and he wasn't going to blow his chance. He just needed to keep his desire for her reined in at the office. But now the question also begged if he could spend time with Hailey outside of work, was it time for him to consider a position with the Navy JAG office? He could still be in the Navy and not be a SEAL, and he decided he owed it to himself to explore the option.

After a grueling morning run, Finn put on his favorite suit and arrived at the office two minutes until eight with a tray of coffee. Hailey's office light was on at the end of the row but he resisted the urge to pop his head in to say good morning. They'd agreed to act normal. He could do normal while he thought of all the things he'd like to try with her once they were done at work.

Instead, he logged onto his computer, bypassing three emails from the senior partners and two clients, opting instead to open one of the emails Hailey had sent at seven a.m. Clearly, he was already failing at acting normal. They were meeting with Mrs. Tovar for an emergency meeting in thirty minutes. But why hadn't Hailey called him? She'd known for an hour something was up.

Before he could get up to ask her, a newspaper fell on his desk.

"Did you see this? She stood before him in a navy-blue suit with a light blue blouse he didn't recall seeing before. His eyes traveled up her frame—the memory of how hungry she had been for his touch and pliant in his arms last night clear in his mind. Her lean muscular form had been responsive to his touch when he ran his hands along every inch of her during their steamy make-out session that had actually fogged up his car windows.

"Good morning, partner. No, I haven't read the paper today. I'm more of a newsfeed on my phone kind of a guy."

"Well, when you're working on a local messy, multimillion-dollar divorce, you may want to scan the local papers on the newsstand."

Her tone was admonishing, but she kept it low so the other rookies wouldn't hear her. And she was correct.

"Okay, fair point." He stood and picked up the paper. "What'd I miss?"

She huffed. "Page two."

Million-Dollar Deal on Sexy Adult-Only Toys the headline read in bold letters at the top of the page.

"She's selling?"

"No, he's trying to."

"What the hell? He knows he can't do that, right?"

"Meet me in the conference room. We only have about twenty minutes before our client is calling in." She grabbed a coffee and silently stalked off. He stepped out into the hallway to place the coffees in a communal area when Smith walked up and grabbed a coffee.

"Damn, Maguire, how can you stand working with such a sweet piece of—"

He didn't even think before knocking the coffee out of Smith's hand, who yelped from the heat of the piping hot brew that burst from the cup and spilled onto the floor.

"You better be more careful what you say. You never know who could overhear you." Finn nodded toward the front doors where Mrs. Stewart and Baxter were approaching.

"Shit, man, thanks."

"Gentlemen, were you fighting for the last cup of coffee?" Baxter said, eyeing the mess.

"No, sir, just a little amped up. I'll have it cleaned up pronto," Smith said, but Finn was already grabbing napkins from his desk to sop up some of the spill.

"Maguire, come see me this afternoon. I need to discuss a new client with you," Baxter said.

"Yes, sir." Damn, his day was really not going well so far. He glanced at his watch. He'd just lost five minutes of prep time, and Hailey would be annoyed, rightfully so. In the conference room, Hailey was already on the phone with their client. He mouthed sorry, and she hit mute.

"She called early. She's really upset." Hailey hit mute again. "Mrs. Tovar, we realize this is extremely upsetting, and you didn't want any of this information hitting the press, which I'm guessing is exactly why your soon-to-be ex-husband is making it such a public issue. But we have already drafted a cease and desist as well as notification to the purchasing company to advise them this business is not for sale. I suspect the buyers are well aware the ownership of this company is being contested and are hoping to get it at a discounted price. The media is just a way to put pressure on you."

"Yes, and it's working. Yesterday, my son said all the kids at school were talking about how his mom probably has a red room. Then he asked what that was. I am humiliated. Maybe I should just cut my losses and let him buy me out."

"Mrs. Tovar," Finn said, "you can obviously do what you

think is best, but we would counsel you against attempting to sell to your ex. For one, I'm guessing your teenage son was less embarrassed than you'd expect, but I do see how this is awkward. If you even hint at an option to sell to your ex, he will fight you for sole ownership even harder, and not pay you a dime. He already claims the company is his. Now is the time to toughen your resolve and not show any weakness."

She exhaled and sniffled over the phone. "He's trying to disrespect me in our community and put a wedge between me and my son. I built this business from scratch and enjoyed the anonymity of quietly creating my own independence away from my terrible choice for a spouse. He always threw in my face that he supported my lifestyle and could easily take it away. My business was my escape from a toxic marriage. And now he's using it to shame me."

"Mrs. Tovar, there is nothing wrong about a woman enjoying pleasure, with or without a partner. There is nothing tawdry or shameful about your business or you. You developed it into a huge success, and it's yours to give away if you think that is the best path. But that won't buy back your anonymity. That's gone. We can shut down this bogus sale and advise the court, but your secret is out. Now you get to decide whether you want to hold your head high and fight for it."

Finn smiled and gave her a thumbs-up. She was passionate and right. Mrs. Tovar's husband had no legal claim to her company.

She huffed over the line. "I didn't want our son to know. I know my ex will try to turn my son against me."

"Talk to your son. I was a tween boy once, and it may surprise you how he's processing all this. Chances are, he doesn't care about the products you make, and he's lost respect for his dad," Finn said.

"I have to say, in our state, your son will soon be old enough to choose who he wants to live with and how often he wants to see the other parent. It's clear you share a much stronger bond with your son than your soon-to-be ex-husband. I realize that isn't what you're after, but your son might feel relieved to know he can choose to stay with you. Empower him to know he doesn't have to be used as a pawn," Hailey offered.

"Okay. I'll speak to my son and see you both in court Monday. Thank you."

"Just call anytime this weekend if something else comes up. We're ready to fight for you, Mrs. Tovar, and that's our plan until you say otherwise," Hailey said.

"I'll let you know if anything changes. Bye."

The phone disconnected, and they both let out a deep breath.

"You were really good with her. I think she needed that push to stick up for herself."

Hailey nodded. "So we have two pieces to file with the court by three today for inclusion in our pre-trial hearing on Monday. Which do you want to do?"

"I thought you said you already had that cease and desist drafted."

"Technically, I do have a blank order open at my desk," she said with a quirk of a smile.

"Well, well, well, maybe you're as tired as I am today and

not quite as fast as I thought with drafting torts."

"I didn't see that story until I arrived, and that was only after Mrs. Tovar texted to ask if I'd seen it."

Finn couldn't help but laugh. "And here I thought you were so hardcore that you'd woke up, put on your superhero cape, found the story, drafted the court order, all before your first cup of coffee," he teased and walked closer but stopped short of touching her.

Her eyes were lit with humor, but she fought the smile that pulled at her sweet, lush lips.

"Don't look at me like you're the big bad wolf getting ready to eat me."

He closed the space between them so his suit brushed against her chest but still didn't break her rule. "I don't know what you mean, Ms. Adams. I was just admiring your ability to manage this case."

She let out a deep breath before biting her lower lip.

"You handle the cease and desist. I'll take on notifying the buyers that Pleasure Inc isn't for sale." She said.

"I'm sorry I wasn't better prepared this morning, but happy to know I wasn't dragging you down."

"Nope, just falling into my trap. Always get to the office before your competition," she said, poking his chest with her finger.

"Let's get lunch after we file these torts with the court," he offered.

Her eyes narrowed.

"I mean a working lunch, discuss our tactics for court on Monday. Or we could swing by my mom's office," he backtracked.

She stepped out of his reach and pulled out a chair in the conference room.

"Okay, I'm going to work here today. All our documents are here, and the bullpen feels more confrontational than usual."

"I agree. I may have smacked a coffee out of Smith's hand earlier."

"Accidentally on purpose?" she asked. "Did he forget to use his internal monologue again?"

"Does he say offensive things to you in the office?" Finn asked, trying to school his annoyance.

She shrugged. "You can't fight my battles, Finn, but yes there are men who think they can treat any woman like a piece of meat, even in the workplace."

"I may not be allowed to fight your battles in the office, but it's inappropriate for him to create a hostile work environment, and I doubt the partners would tolerate it if they were privy to it."

"Finn, we agreed, strictly professional."

He gritted his teeth and nodded. "I have to see Baxter, something about a new client. But then I'll complete my tort and see you for lunch. One o'clock?"

"Okay."

He didn't want to leave, and he didn't want to pretend he wasn't seething to learn that Smith had been harassing her and probably every woman in the bullpen for the last year. It had only been a week of working together, but in truth, he'd felt tied to Hailey for two years. Before he'd admired her beauty and intelligence, now she was more than just a colleague; she was special to him already. Of course he wanted to protect her. And he wanted to spend as much time with her after work as possible. It was Friday, and he hoped she would agree to spend some of the weekend with him. He knew she often worked on the weekends, but what else did she do?

On his way up the elevator, he decided exactly where they could go to spend time together, his family's lake cabin. At the lake, they could be alone and wouldn't run into anyone in the city.

With a new spring in his step, his shoes made a clacking sound along the marble floors as he walked through the senior partners' lobby. He stopped outside Mr. Baxter's door.

"Come on in," Mr. Baxter said and patted him on the back.

Finn was surprised to see Admiral Maddox sitting relaxed in a chair across from Baxter's desk. The man stood and also shook Finn's hand before they all took a seat. Maddox was in his late fifties but carried himself like you'd expect a man who had served twenty years in the military, ten on an elite team, and built a multimillion-dollar business from scratch. He wore a fitted polished suit, perfectly shined shoes, but nothing else that said money. No flashy watch or shiny cufflinks. Simple, impeccable style.

"Finn, I'm appointing you to take lead on a legal matter Mr. Maddox is having that requires discretion. We both know you'll maintain the privacy of attorney-client privilege, but this is delicate," Mr. Baxter said.

Leaning forward, Mr. Maddox steepled his fingers together and met Finn's gaze.

"I'm looking for someone, but I'm not very confident we'll find them. I've hired a private investigator, but he's run into several legal issues. I'd rather not use my usual firm that handles my business engagements for reasons that will become obvious.

"I have reason to believe I fathered a child twenty-eight years ago, and I intend to leave her an inheritance."

Finn was surprised by the story Mr. Maddox was telling but schooled his features to remain neutral.

"I'd be happy to handle any legal documents to create a trust in absentia. Although, I'd counsel you to have a backup plan if you can't find the child, or woman. What exactly did you plan to leave her?"

Mr. Maddox stood and walked to the windows. "I don't have any other children. I never married. So I'd like to leave her my life's work. A pathetic attempt to apologize for not being there for her."

Finn doubted his shock was written all over his face. The man was worth almost fifty million, having turned his engineering degree and experience in close quarters combat into sensor technology that was patented and snapped up by the leading manufacturer of drones for commercial use.

"If you put me in touch with your PI, I'll see where the case has run cold and if we can make any additional progress. You may want to include the requirement of a DNA test for the heir, in order to confirm."

Mr. Maddox nodded. "Yes, Baxter has lectured me all about the dangers of false claims."

"Should I also vet the source, Mr. Maddox? Perhaps the child's mother found out about your success and is just claiming there was a child?" Finn said.

"You don't really need all the sordid details, but suffice it to say, a woman I spent time with between deployments had a child. But she never claimed me as the father because she was married to another soldier when she discovered the pregnancy. Fast-forward, the destructive marriage ended, the mother died, and a child bounced around to a few homes before she ran away or maybe worse."

"Sir, what makes you think the story is true or that you could still find her?" Finn had to ask.

"The child's maternal grandmother sent me a letter, claiming I was the father of her grandchild five years ago. I'd been deployed on my last tour in Iraq at the time, and the woman's health was failing her. By the time I could meet with her she was living in a nursing home after a terrible stroke, so she wasn't able to communicate. The facility wouldn't give me any information about a next of kin, and the woman died. I did confirm her daughter had been a woman I thought I loved once. The PI managed to track down the child by birth records, but when her mom died, it wasn't clear who raised her or what name she was going by."

"I'm sorry you missed out on knowing her, but I'll do my best to create a trust in case the private investigators can find her."

"Thank you, and I appreciate your attention to how delicate this is. If my board at Maddox Corp. finds out I want to leave the majority of my wealth to a child I've never met, I'm afraid there could be a mutiny. I just can't help but think maybe one day my daughter will figure it out and come looking for me. But mostly I just need to know if she's ever found out that I didn't completely abandon her."

Finn could see the admiral was distressed by what could have happened to his own child. He didn't really need to press for any more information. It was sad, but he doubted Mr. Maddox would ever know what happened to his child.

"I'll draw up the documents and call you directly to review them once it's done."

"Very good, Finn," Mr. Baxter said, standing. It was time for Finn to go.

"Mr. Maddox, I'll be in touch early next week."

A new case was the last thing he needed, but it was obvious why Maddox had chosen him. The military community was strong, but on the SEAL team, the brotherhood was for life. They were men forever linked in training, battle, and war. Finn hoped for Maddox's sake that the power of some legal court requests would reveal more information and help him find his daughter. Now he had a new reason to stay on at the firm while he worked with Hailey on their joint case. But he intended to put a call into the Navy JAG office on Monday.

Chapter Ten

Hailey

SOMETHING WAS OFF. Hailey's focus was gone. Her skin tingled, and she had enough energy to run at least a 10k—and she didn't even like to run. She'd finished her notification to the firm attempting to buy Mrs. Tovar's company, and now she was impatiently waiting until one o'clock to see Finn. Her eager need to see him was unprofessional. Not to mention unnerving. She'd been so independent for so long, unable to count on anyone or let herself want anything from anyone.

She'd had a few acquaintances in college, classmates she'd studied with, but between school, working, and caring for her grandmother, she didn't have much time. Friendships always seemed like a lot of extra work, and people would get nosy about her past. Boyfriends were a bit easier, more surface companionships. They provided company and met physical needs, but if they got clingy, she just moved on. Which would explain why she'd only had two real boyfriends and both were short-lived.

Since living in Alexandria, she hadn't dated at all. She worked all the time. She was beginning to realize how sad that was. There was being driven and then there was being an obsessive hermit. The funny thing was, men often did ask her for her phone number at the grocery store or in the coffee shop near her place. One guy who worked at the courthouse had pursued her a bit, but she'd told him she wasn't available. She was married to her ambition and chasing the junior partnership.

"Hey, are you ready to review my work?" Finn appeared in the doorway of her office. "I saved it in the shared folder for our case."

His suit jacket was off, and his sleeves were cuffed up to reveal his tan forearms with a sprinkle of tawny hair that she itched to touch. Maybe he was the right guy to break her dry spell. Their chemistry was off the charts, but it was in complete conflict with her policy to never date anyone at work. Although if it was just hooking up, after hours, to relieve this pressure between them, then it wasn't really dating. And if she made partner, she would just end it because there was no way she could expect the other rookies to respect her if she was sleeping with one of them. Sex—she had just acknowledged that she wanted to have sex with Finn.

He stepped farther into her tiny office, his eyes studying her as if he could read her mind.

"You okay? You look like you just figured something out," he asked in a low tone.

"Yes. I'll take a look and meet you in the bullpen," she said, opening her laptop and squeezing her legs together.

She'd just given herself permission to have Finn, but first they needed to file these documents with the court. It was

Friday, and once they were done at the courthouse, they could easily get away with not returning to the office. It was out of character for her and it was probably going to backfire, but she was long overdue for some fun. Finn's hot body and charming nature seemed like just the right type of fun she needed.

After a quick review, she printed both their documents and tucked her laptop into her bag in case she didn't make it back to the office. Finn met her near the elevators.

"All good?" he asked.

"Yep, just excited to file these."

He nodded and held the doors open for her. Two other people on the elevator moved to the side, and Finn followed her in, forced to stand in front of her. The elevator stopped on the next floor, and the two strangers got off. Finn slid to the side just as the doors closed and stood quietly.

A moment later, she reached out and hit the stop button on the elevator. Just like in the movies, it shook to a stop, and an alarm went off.

"Hailey, what are you doing?"

She dropped her bag and stepped in front of him. Pushing her hand inside his suit jacket, she could feel his carved muscular back. She stood on her tiptoes while her other hand looped behind his neck, pulling his mouth down to meet hers.

His surprise gave her the upper hand as she licked her tongue into his mouth. He tasted like sugar and cinnamon. But in the next second, his reaction was visceral. His hands gripped her hips and hoisted her legs up around his narrow waist. Next he pushed her back against the wall of the elevator. He met her tongue with steady pressure before moving his lips down her throat.

"You must either be a mind reader, or you've been wanting this as much as me," he breathed.

His morning shave had grown out just enough for the tiny hairs to rub along her skin as his mouth dipped lower into the neckline of her button-down blouse. His strong hands held her up as she bounced her hips, feeling his hard desire pressed against her. His mouth was back on hers; one hand held her neck in a gentle but dominating way that she was surprised to find she liked. His thumb stroked her chin as they tasted and teased each other.

The sound of a phone ringing broke through the haze of desire he was creating. He stopped kissing her but didn't move away. They both took several labored breaths.

"Shoot, I hope there isn't a camera in here," she said.

Finn's mouth pressed against her collarbone in one more hot, open-mouth kiss. His tongue tasted her before he pulled back enough to look into her eyes.

"I'm going to restart the elevator. We're going to straighten our clothes and walk out of here like two mature adults."

Chest heaving, she nodded, unable to form any coherent response.

Steadying her against the wall, he ran a hand over his suit, which had been crumpled in their haste. Then he released the stop button on the elevator, handed her the bag she'd discarded, and pulled her blazer together as they continued their descent to the lobby. The phone stopped ringing.

"Snap out of it. One walk across the lobby, and we can take my car to the courthouse."

How was he so focused and unaffected by what had just passed between them? Seconds before, he had been just as desperate to touch her as she'd been to feel his warm, muscular body.

"Yep, okay." She nodded and kept her eyes down, running her fingers over what felt like swollen recently kissed lips.

"You look fine," he breathed. "Gorgeous and sexy but still like a professional lawyer."

She looked up and recognized the desire that shone bright in his eyes just before the elevator doors opened.

She practically ran off the elevator and nearly plowed into several rookies coming back from lunch.

"Slow down, Hailey. We all get it. You're dedicated," Smith sneered.

She stopped in her tracks and turned. He was always making rude comments and trying to use his broad shoulders to intimidate people, as if it made up for his poor skills as a lawyer. He was a condescending bully.

"And we all know that as soon as I make partner, you're toast. So you should spend more time on your resumé and less time being rude." Then she stalked off toward the garage. But she could hear a few of the rookies snickering at her truthful comments.

Finn caught up to her in the dimly lit concrete stairwell where she'd paused to catch her breath. What was getting into her? First she jumped Finn, then she told her nemesis how much he sucked.

"That was epic. Who are you, and what have you done with Hailey Adams?" Finn said before placing his hand on the small of her back and ushering her to his car in the second row.

"I guess I just hit my wall."

He didn't say anything about their kiss, and she couldn't decide if she was disappointed or relieved.

She resisted the urge to kiss him again as he opened the car door for her. They drove to the courthouse in silence through the busy afternoon traffic. After filing the documents, they made their way back to his car, and he headed out of the city. Although she was curious where they were going, she didn't want to have to ask. The truth was, she'd go anywhere with him. A thought that excited and terrified her. But she didn't want to have to ask him—she wanted him to figure it out.

Finally, about twenty minutes outside the city, he pulled over next to a quaint old diner in a small town.

"Are you hungry?"

"Starved."

His smile quirked up on one side. "Good. We can eat and talk. I don't want you making any rash decisions on an empty stomach. We both know you'll just get hangry."

She smiled. He was right. Not only would her blood sugar spike dangerously low, but she also got testy when she didn't eat regularly.

The diner was busy with what appeared to be a school field trip. She and Finn looked like D.C. castaways in their suits, but no one paid them any attention. Finn asked for a booth, but this time he was forced to sit across from her at a narrow table for two.

"They have great burgers and corn dogs."

"I've never had a corn dog, but a burger sounds good," she said, looking at the menu.

"Never?"

"I didn't grow up like you. There were no trips to restaurants or quaint diners."

"Okay, so tell me about how you grew up."

She lifted her gaze, unsure what to say. She now understood what a deer in the headlights felt like. There was nowhere to run or hide as Finn's cool green eyes watched her.

"You don't really want to hear about my messed-up childhood, and I don't want to talk about it."

He reached across the table and gripped her hand, and she didn't fight him. The warm, smooth touch of his skin was welcomed and sent a ripple of need through her. She'd been blissfully unaware that her body was lonely until Finn touched her.

"The thing is, I do want to hear about your life, and I think you probably need to talk about it. Have you ever told anyone what happened?"

She eyed him warily.

"No, it's never come up. Sure, people ask the generic 'where are you from?' question," she scoffed, glancing over his shoulder but not really seeing the rambunctious kids in the background. "People want a bland answer to that loaded question. They don't want to hear about a little girl tossed around in foster care suffering different types of mistreatment in every home until she runs away."

"Or you've gotten so good at deflecting that you've dodged the questions and concerns over the years."

Huffing, she gazed over at the pies in the glass case across from them but stayed quiet.

"Okay. You don't have to tell me anything, but I'm not going to let you decide all the terms of this relationship in a vacuum."

Her eyes flew back to meet his. "Relationship?"

"Yes." A slow smile formed on his mouth, and he squeezed her hand. "Relationship. When two consenting adults like each other and enjoy each other's company so they decide to spend time together. It's called a relationship."

She squirmed in her seat. Thankfully, the waitress arrived, but Finn quickly ordered a half dozen items and the woman left to get their drinks. Leaning forward, he waited for Hailey to meet his eyes.

"If you think I'm just going to hook up with you and follow you around in court like a puppy, you've got the wrong guy."

"I never asked you to follow me around."

"No, but you assume you're in charge of our case and our relationship because you're used to calling all the shots in your life."

"Hello pot, I think I'm the kettle."

He nodded. "I'm capable of letting you take the lead, as long as I get a say. It's a partnership in my mind."

"I'm not good at that. I don't know how to trust that you won't mess up this case or screw me over to get partner."

"I get that, but I'm asking you to please try. I won't screw you over for anything."

She fiddled with her napkin with one hand as his other hand remained steady, settled over hers, forcing her to feel the comfort he offered.

"And the relationship, what does that mean to you?" she dared to ask.

"Same thing. You trust me to honor you, care for your feelings, and you do likewise for me. I'm not asking you to relive every dark day in your past, but I would like to know you better. This beguiling beauty you try so hard to hide and that brilliant mind for the law didn't just come from nowhere."

Hailey took a deep breath.

"I was born in Virginia, but we moved when I was little for my dad's work to North Carolina. My parents' marriage was volatile, and my dad walked out on my mom, a lot. The last time he didn't come back and my mom fell apart. She died young with no family in the area, and I ended up in foster care. I was nine."

She paused, recognizing concern in Finn's eyes. He gave her hand a squeeze, and she took a sip of her water before continuing.

"Foster care is as bad as you can imagine. At sixteen, after my foster dad treated my arm like a torture experiment, I ran away. But I knew I had a grandmother in Virginia so I made my way back to the one address I'd seen in my file and she was living in a rundown house. She needed help and I needed a place to stay off the streets, which were scarier than foster care. Gran let me stay, and I made myself useful. Once I turned eighteen I didn't have to hide from foster care and got my GED."

The air seemed thick, and she avoided his eyes, not wanting to see the pity or disgust in his gorgeous face.

"I don't like how people treat me once they know I was thrown away in foster care. Like I'm damaged goods. Or some charity case."

Finn gripped her hand. "I don't think that. I think you're a warrior, a survivor. You're the most intelligent and passionate lawyer I've met, but that isn't even the most interesting part about you to me."

Daring to meet his eyes, she didn't see pity. It was more like a fire of need.

"I want nothing more than to learn all your secrets so I can feel closer to you and guard them for you. Maybe then you can let them go and open up to me more."

"You do?"

"Yes, and it's not just because I find you insanely beautiful but I'm drawn to you, like a puzzle piece I didn't know was missing. I crave you, Hailey. Every day, I wake up excited to see you, and every night, I replay what we did together, wondering if you're feeling this vibe between us too."

"You do?" She was gobsmacked. No one had ever made her feel so desirable before. Finn was so open with what he wanted, and his words pushed the need she had for him to the surface.

Before he could respond, their waitress appeared with plates piled high: corn dogs, sliders, fries, milk, and a bowl of brussels sprouts. Then she was gone.

"Why the brussels sprouts?"

"We're going to relieve some childhood rites of passage,

one of which is having to eat your vegetables."

Laughing, she took a small sip of her huge milk. Her cheeks ached from smiling so much, and she couldn't think of anyone else in her life who ever knew what she needed before she did.

"I like you, too, but I have no idea how to be in a real relationship. I don't even know what that is."

Finn nodded.

"We start with honesty and getting to know each other, more kissing, and then we'll see. If you eat your lunch, I'll take you to my favorite place ever since I was a kid."

She picked up the stick with the crispy corn dog and took a big bite.

"I can do that," she said as she chewed.

During lunch and their drive, Finn carried the conversation while taking advantage of every chance to touch her. It was a gesture of familiarity and comfort. Their dynamic had shifted—the farther they got out of the city, the more relaxed she became. City streets were a far cry from the lush tree-lined two-lane state road they traveled.

"Almost there," Finn said, breaking through her thoughts.

She watched outside the window as he took a right turn down a more narrow road with bushes crowding the path. A few homes were visible in the trees until the view opened up to reveal a big lake. Greenish-blue crests of the water sparkled in the late afternoon sun.

"Where are we?"

"Lake Anna. My grandfather built a cabin out here in the sixties. Ever since I was a kid, my family's been coming here every chance we got during the summer and holidays."

Riveted, she watched the idyllic, huge, mirrored lake through the window as Finn drove along the windy road. The water was surrounded by majestic tall trees and lush thick grass.

"Every summer?"

"For a few weeks when my parents could take the time off at least."

"No wonder you're a SEAL. I can barely tread water."

"Oh, well you're in luck because I can teach you. You'd be surprised how many kids who can't swim join the Navy."

She whipped her head around to find him smiling before he pulled the car off the main road and parked in a stone driveway under the shade of more trees.

"So we're not going back to the office today?" she asked.

"Not unless you want to."

"Nope." She surprised herself by replying without hesitation.

Across the lawn, a well-used deck jutted out to the water. Beyond that was an island platform bobbing in the gentle waves. The home was framed by a white picket fence, white shutters on a gray cabin, with a friendly red door.

"This looks nicer than a cabin."

Finn laughed and unbuckled his belt.

"My folks upgraded over time, and then a few years ago, when my dad retired, the big remodel happened. He calls it the posh cabin now—my mom calls it their oasis."

"Oasis looks about right. I think it'd be hard to go back to the city if you knew you had this waiting for you."

"Come on." He opened his door and got out.

Taking a deep breath, she caught sight of her reflection in the glass window of her passenger door. She was about to do something very uncharacteristic of herself and just have fun with a man she worked with and happened to be extremely attracted to. She was going to let her guard down and enjoy every moment with Finn.

Chapter Eleven

Finn

BRINGING HAILEY TO his family cabin seemed like the most natural thing. Even more surprising was her willingness to go and the casual agreement to blow off going back to the office. Did she feel the intimacy of being alone with him at his family lake house?

After unlocking the door, he ushered her into one of the first rooms off the open, airy nautical-themed entryway.

"So in this guest room, we keep extra bathing suits."

He walked over to the top drawer of the dresser and found a few women's suits with tags still on them. "My mom keeps the cabin well stocked for guests." Hailey remained standing by the doorway. Her lawyerly business suit was a complete contrast to the cozy room with aqua walls, white bunk beds, and a matching dresser. She looked so serious. "Choose whichever one you like, and you can change in the en suite. I have a suit in another room. Meet me out back."

She took a step closer but just shy of the plush shag rug on the floor.

"We're really going swimming?"

"Yes, the lake will be warmed from the sun, perfect for

your first lesson, and if you do a good job listening, we can do sparklers before dinner."

She kicked off her pumps and took a few more steps closer.

"Sparklers?"

He had every intention of not touching her, but it was like she put him in a trance. Closing the space between them, he slid his arms around her small waist.

"Yes, we're going to enjoy some childhood pleasures you missed out on. Then after the sun sets, you can decide if you need to go home or want to stay the night," he said, careful to watch the reaction in her blue eyes that looked like the sky right before a thunderstorm.

She leaned up and kissed him gently, her soft lips torturing him and instantly sending a rush of excitement through him. Pressing her body into his, she slipped her hands up along his neck to pull his mouth closer before ending the kiss.

"Can we explore some adult pleasures before our swimming lesson?"

Her mouth was back on his before he could respond, and their mutual desire exploded with a frenzy.

Clothes went flying, hands exploring, and mouths tasting. He discovered several old scars marring her creamy skin, and he held her eyes as he kissed those too. Soon her lean form covered in only a simple set of cotton panties and a matching bra stood before him. Reaching up, she pulled her long hair free from the conservative knot at the base of her neck, and the whitish-blond hair pooled around her shoulders.

Neither of them spoke.

He kissed every angle until he was kneeling in front of her, where his mouth found her toned abs, and he watched as her chest rose and fell. She tried to catch her breath and pushed her hands through his. Her nails tickled his scalp, and he shivered looking up into her eyes glossy with desire.

"We don't have to do anything more if you're not ready," he said.

Slowly, she stepped back and then sank to her knees, meeting him on the plush rug.

"I couldn't deny either of us this even if I wanted to," she said before laying back and spreading her legs. Then she reached for him.

Careful not to put his full weight on her lithe frame, he hovered above her, tracing the line of her collarbone with his mouth.

"You're beautiful, babe," he said in her ear and felt her subtly shake her head to disagree.

"You are to me—these long, lean, feminine legs, strong arms, lush pink lips, and your stubborn brilliant mind." He ran his hand down the line of muscle along her arm, over her hip, then cupped between her legs and applied pressure with the ball of his palm. At the same time, he leaned forward to gently kiss her lips between each word.

"You're perfect, and I have never wanted a woman more. I'm going to show you just how special you are to me, Hailey."

He took his time stroking, licking, kissing, and coaxing her body into a bucking and convulsing ball of need.

"More, I want more from you," she begged.

Standing, he chucked his suit pants and briefs as she writhed on the ground waiting for him. Then without hesitation he kneeled again between her legs and with painful restraint hooked his fingers into her panties to pull them down her long limbs. In desperation she removed her bralette with haste, revealing herself to him, in all her glory. She was more than beautiful; she was everything he wanted and needed.

"More, Finn," she begged, pulling him on top of her and hooking her legs around his waist.

"Okay, babe, I'll give you everything you want. Anything you want."

With one tediously slow plunge, he was inside her, and they both released the breath they were holding. His mouth was on hers as the rush of his desire for her was overpowered by the sense of something profound. She needed him as much as he needed her, and it was clear it went beyond desire.

Like a dance they'd choreographed and practiced—their bodies moved together. Balancing his weight on one elbow, he hovered above her and held her gaze, watching her mouth gasp with each thrust, and reveling in the pleasure she took from him. Her hands smoothed over his shoulders, and her nails skimmed his back as she rocked her hips to meet him. They were soaring toward complete ecstasy, and he never wanted to let her go. But she was holding back, so he pushed harder, releasing her stare. He kissed her neck and stroked her body until she was yelling out his name, and he met her in a burst of pleasure he felt with every ounce of his being.

With his heart pounding, Finn lay back on the floor,

staring up at the ceiling. They were both still breathing heavily as their skin cooled. Naked and spent, Hailey pressed her hand into his, and she squeezed it before turning her head to the side to face him.

"I like your cabin," she said.

Laughing, he rolled onto his side, propped up his head, and let his eyes skim down her figure.

"I like it even more now." He let his fingers lightly trace down from the dent of her clavicle to the middle of her chest before tracing the lines of her abs.

"Are you ready for that swim now?" he asked.

"Yes." Her eyes had closed when he began to touch her, but they popped open again. "Can we stay here tonight?"

"If you want to, we could stay here forever and just become lake bums."

"Oh, that sounds like low stress. What would we do all day?"

The playful twinkle in her eyes was new, and he liked it. Leaning forward, he kissed her gently as his hand stroked along her thigh, over the curve of her hip, and up to frame her delicate jaw. As he pulled back, he spotted goose bumps speckling her body.

"Kissing, naked Tuesday's, and the occasional visit from family—then you would need clothes."

"Hmmm, solid plan. I'll think about it."

Her blue eyes remained fixed on him but crinkled on the sides, and her lips were fighting a smile. She was happy and relaxed, two feelings he would guess she didn't let herself feel too often. The sudden need to make her happy indefinitely pulsed through him. Was he capable of capturing her heart and keeping it?

Today he had her, and he wasn't going to let either of them miss it.

"What is it?" she asked as she studied him.

"You just make me happy, and I don't mean just because we had epic sex on the floor of my cabin." Pressing his lips to hers, he didn't let her respond.

Deepening the kiss, he gripped her hip and pulled her to roll on top of him as he lay back. Her lean form covered him, and the weight of her breasts pressed against his chest. A lightning-fast arousal throbbed between them.

"You're as insatiable as I feel," she said, pulling her knees up on either side of his hips and pushing herself to sit up and hover above him.

Her white-blonde hair cascaded down, tickling his skin as she leaned forward and kissed him with a smile. Then in one swift movement, she lifted her hips up, only to envelope him inside her heat and sank back down.

A hiss escaped his mouth at the feel of pure pleasure she created.

"You're spectacularly sexy," he said as he skimmed his hands over her legs and up her back.

"You're not so bad yourself," she said breathlessly as they both began to rock against the tide of need building.

She pressed one pebbled peak of her breast over his lips, and he needed no further encouragement. Sucking the hard nub into his mouth, his teeth skimmed the sensitive skin, causing her to groan.

"We may not make it back to the city until Sunday," she warned, and her hips rocked faster over him.

Her head fell back, dangling her hair down, and he sat up to hold her closer. Meeting her tempo with pressure between their bodies rubbing and stroking. He could feel her body stiffen and watched a fissure of pleasure pulse through her, right before his own release. She collapsed against him breathing hard, and her skin was covered in a sheen of sweat. He fell back, carrying her down with him, and enjoyed the languid weight of her over his chest. Even now, his body twitched with eager desire for her. With one hand, he gave her butt a firm smack—and then froze.

"Babe, I'm sorry. Did I hurt you?" he asked, waiting to see her reaction.

But the sound of her laugh met his fear that maybe she didn't like to have her juicy round bottom swatted, even playfully during sex. Her body vibrated on his as she peeked up at him.

"I'm fine, and yes, I liked it. I know you won't hurt me."

"Okay, I just don't want to cross any lines."

She shut him up with a kiss before hopping up and pulling his hands to force him to stand.

"Let's go for that swim," she said, ending any conversation about what was safe in the bedroom.

She found a green one piece that still had the tags on, and he dug out his yellow trunks in the other room, where she found him.

"Is this your usual room?" she asked, stepping into the well-lit cozy space. There were sailboat prints in black-and-white, and one wall was covered in a deep royal blue. A queen-size bed, a tall bookshelf, and cozy chair in the corner were all the room offered.

He couldn't help but smile. "Sort of. This is the healing room."

"Healing?"

"Yah, when I returned from a long deployment, I would come here and just rest. My mom said it was healing because I was always in a better mood after a few nights out here."

She stepped into his arms and hugged him around his waist and squeezed.

"This will be your suit now," he said, noticing the kelly-green material was cut low in the back with a crisscross of straps. He couldn't keep his hands off her and started to move her closer toward the door. "We better get out of this house before I change my mind. We only have about an hour left of light. Then I'll make dinner."

"Are you trying to butter me up so I'll let you take the lead in court on Monday?"

"No, I'm trying to butter you up so you'll sleep in that bed with me later."

Her laugh rang through the empty house as he flipped on a light, and she seemed to grow self-conscious all of a sudden standing in the kitchen in only her bathing suit, looking like his fantasy come-to life. She crossed her arms over her chest, and he noticed the smattering of old scars along her beautiful skin.

"No, no, no, you can't be bashful with me. Not after I've kissed every inch of you." Wrapping his arms around her, he kissed her eyes then her mouth. "No hiding with me."

She nodded.

"Alright, so when was the last time you went swimming?" he asked, grabbing a few towels from a hidden bench in the bay window by the French doors leading to the deck.

"Do you count being tossed in a pool and flailing to the edge to survive? That was in college, the one and only time I attempted to attend a party."

He fought the anger that bubbled up at the idea of anyone putting their hands on her and tossing someone unable to swim into the pool.

"You made it out, so yes. But we're going to start with the basics, and at no time will you be in any danger, okay?"

"Okay, coach." Her smile confirmed she believed him.

She wouldn't be in any danger, but he was in danger of losing his heart.

Chapter Twelve

Hailey

THE COLD WATER was soothing to her tender skin. After she'd rolled around on the floor with Finn, her knees were sore, and her body felt fatigued but in a good way, like Finn's kisses washed away any old wounds. She hadn't slept with anyone in years, and sex had never felt as intimate as it had when her body was joined with Finn's. It wasn't just the physical act. He saw her. He immersed her in affection and cherished her body. If it weren't so foolish, she would say he made love to her, but she had no idea what that would really entail and they weren't in love. Lust was a given.

No one else had ever made her feel so safe or given her so much pleasure.

Now as she floated on her back in the lake under Finn's watchful eye, she felt it again—secure, knowing he would protect her as well as a desire for him that was unwavering.

"Good, I want you to always trust you can survive in the water, at any depth, by floating on your back," Finn said with steady confidence. "Now, slowly drop your feet to the floor and stand."

She did as directed and discovered the water was only up

to her hips.

"Next, let's try blowing some bubbles and dunking our heads."

She followed his lead and was content to let her guard down completely. She listened, and by the end of the hour, they swam, or doggy paddled to the diving platform farther out in the lake. He stayed next to her the entire way.

When she made it to the side, she was out of breath, and her limbs were like Jell-O.

"You're a fast learner," Finn said.

"I don't like failure."

"No kidding." He laughed. "I wouldn't have guessed that about you."

She splashed water at him and rested her head on the side of the platform.

"Watch how to hoist yourself out and be careful of the edge."

In one graceful movement, he pulled himself up and out of the water. The muscles on his back flexed, and his biceps bulged into thick balls while each sinewy line of his forearms stood at attention. His body was a piece of art.

She fell back into the water on her first attempt but got the motion of propelling herself up and made it out of the water before collapsing on the wood planks with her legs still hanging over on one side. Her chest heaved with the expulsion of the rest of her energy.

His boyish smile made her heart skip a beat, and he rewarded her with a kiss as he leaned over her. Before she knew it, he had her panting and clawing at his back. In one swift move, she flipped him onto his back and straddled him, her new favorite position.

"Okay, clearly you have more hidden talents to share," he said, pulling down the straps of her suit before placing his mouth over her chilled skin.

Her need for him mounted as she rocked over his hard desire clearly defined in his wet trunks. With assured speed, he pushed down his trunks and pulled her bathing suit bottom to the side before joining their bodies ever so slowly. They both let out a cry of pure animalistic satisfaction. His mouth was on her throat, and he propped himself up using one hand to support him and the other behind her back.

"I can't get enough," he breathed. "I want to be closer to you, I want all of you."

His words were like a medicine she didn't know she needed. He was awakening a part of her she didn't recognize. Their bodies moved with a familiarity of each other. With her arms looped around his shoulders, she continued to rock slowly, savoring him, shivering from the sensations swirling over her. Both his arms wrapped around her back now, cradling her neck and pulling her shoulders down in rhythm with his hips. His kisses were languid and sweet, and she didn't realize she was crying until his thumb wiped at her cheek. The sun had almost set, and the pinks and reds cast just enough light for her to see the question in his eyes. But she silenced him with a kiss because she didn't have an answer. She didn't know what was happening between them, and she wasn't ready to figure it out.

Maybe sex with Finn was making her fall apart, but it was too late to worry about it now.

When she exploded into a million pieces on his lap, he

held her and drew out her orgasm before finding his own. She shivered against a cool breeze on her back, and he finally spoke into the dark.

"I think we just flew past getting to know each other."

Afraid to say anything, she leaned back and pulled up her bathing suit straps before standing. Adjusting his trunks, he stood and took both her hands in his.

"For the record, I want to be more than your colleague or your competition," Finn said, "in case there is any doubt on where I stand."

For the first time, he was shy and hesitant with his words, as if he had no idea he already owned her body. Maybe more.

"Okay, but that doesn't change that we are colleagues and in competition for a partnership."

His hand moved up her neck, and she thought he was going to say he didn't care about the partnership and he only wanted her, but he didn't. Instead, he smiled but it didn't meet his eyes.

"After we win this case next week, the partners will have to decide on the junior partnership. Then you won't have any excuses and nowhere to hide from this connection between us."

"Who is hiding? I just straddled you outside and screamed your name."

"You know what I mean," he said and patted her bottom.

"Finn, if I get selected for partner, I can't be sleeping with one of the rookie's I'm managing. And if I don't get partner, I'm not staying with the firm."

"You're going to quit if you don't win?"

She gulped. "Everyone knows if you don't get partner by year five, it means you're not the right fit at Baxter and Stewart."

"It's not going to matter because they would be fools not to select you. And lately, I've been considering a move anyway."

"You have?"

"I miss the Navy, but not as a SEAL. I put in a call to the local JAG office to discuss my options."

"You want to go back to the military?"

"I think so."

"You can't tell Baxter and Stewart until they decide on the partnership. I need to know if I win based on my work, not as a default if you quit."

He nodded and kissed her chin. "Okay, I won't say anything until the case is won, and they announce the winner of the partnership. I just want you to know that I'm not playing any game. No matter what, I want you."

He kissed her before she could feel forced to respond, and the only thing she could think to do was jump into the water. She didn't have the heart to tell him that she wasn't going to stay in the area if it wasn't at Baxter and Stewart. She couldn't risk him telling them he didn't want the partnership. She needed to know she was good enough. Finn followed through the water and didn't bring it up again. Not when he wrapped her in a plush towel on the shore or explored her body in the hot shower. With every adoring stroke, he forced her to wonder what it would be like to be with Finn. No limits, no hiding.

That evening, after a delicious dinner of pasta and a homemade sauce from the freezer, Finn led her to the living room couch. And they did something she'd never done: they snuggled under a blanket to watch a movie. He pretended to be appalled at her lack of knowledge on action movies and rom-coms then forced her to watch his all-time favorite movie, *Goonies.* They both fell asleep at some point, but she stirred when he carried her to bed, feeling the full power of letting someone care for her. In the morning, the sound of his steady breathing and the heat from his body enveloped her. Under the covers, lying next to Finn, she was warm, safe, and cozy. A combination she hadn't experienced since childhood. Her short relationships had always seemed transactional, each person wanting something from the other.

Finn said he wanted her no matter what happened with the partnership. He was so outspoken about his feelings, but it meant she had to consider what they were doing beyond the moment.

But if she did win, they couldn't be together. There was no policy per se against them dating, but the perception would be favoritism; the junior partner typically took over the management of the rookie bullpen, assisting with case assignments and firing the poor performers.

"Shh, you're thinking too much," Finn whispered as his hand slowly pushed under her arm and pulled her back into his body.

His firm mass of muscles pressed against her back, stirring a fresh craving in her.

"There you go. It's too early to be tense. Let me see if I

can help you relax again." His mouth was on her ear, and she arched into him enjoying his manly impulse and instant need for her. No matter what happened with the partnership, she was going to enjoy every fleeting moment with him until the end.

✕

AFTER WHAT COULD only be described as the most romantic weekend of her life, a cloud settled over Hailey. Early Sunday morning, they got back in the car to return to the city.

"Will you come with me to family dinner tonight, or do you need a break from me?"

Gripping his hand, she couldn't help but smile.

"I think I need time to prepare for court and probably a refresher on how not to kiss you every five minutes."

"Nah, you can kiss me in court—it's fine."

His lopsided sly grin, accentuated by the two days of scruff, made him look beyond sexy and completely threatening to her need to maintain some space.

"I'm just teasing. I won't push my luck, but when we're done in court each day, you're mine."

"Okay, are you going to the office today?"

"Of course. We can't win this case on my Maguire charm."

"It's probably worth a shot. You're very charming."

"Finally, she admits she finds me charming."

"Charming, handsome, and maybe a glutton for misfits."

"You're not a misfit. Don't sell yourself short."

Nodding, she couldn't help but wish he was right. But

the gnawing fear of being alone again or rejected sat like a stone in her stomach. The easiest way to avoid those feelings was to never count on someone. As soon as she expected someone to be there for her, she was opening herself up for the fall.

Swallowing the stifling feeling that she was already in trouble with her emotions when it came to Finn, she pulled her hand away to grab her water.

"I actually need to head into the office. I have a new case I need to draft some paperwork on, then I can focus on our case. Or vice versa," he said, breaking through her tumbling thoughts.

"Okay. Can you drop me off at my place, and I'll meet you there? I need some fresh clothes."

"My T-shirt you're wearing is fresh."

"Very funny."

"I can grab us some breakfast while you get dressed, and we can go to the office together."

Hesitating, she squirmed in her seat but felt the shift in the air.

"Oh, I get it. You don't want to risk anyone seeing us roll into the office together on a Sunday."

Before she could respond, his phone rang, interrupting the awkward silence, but he let the call go to voicemail when he didn't recognize the number.

"I explained this could only work outside the office. That hasn't changed. It's different for you. Men don't get the same scrutiny women do when they sleep with someone at work."

He nodded. "You're right. You did tell me how it was

going to be. I don't like it, but I understand."

But the question on what happened when one of them made partner hung in the air. They had one hot, amazing weekend, and everything was jumbled in her mind. She didn't want to think about what would happen next with them.

She needed to focus on winning their case.

Chapter Thirteen

Finn

HAILEY'S NEED TO compartmentalize their personal relationship from their professional one was smart. Finn understood and agreed, but he still hated it and couldn't help but be disappointed. Knowing it was only temporary while the partnership at work was finalized helped.

Once he dropped her off, he listened to the voicemail he'd gotten on the drive, from the private investigator for the Admiral Maddox case. The PI wanted to discuss the details he'd gathered, so Finn called him right back.

It was clear the investigator had hit a brick wall after tracking down the grandmother's previous addresses. The trail on the child had gone cold, and the Department of Children Services wasn't helpful due to poor records and privacy claims. Except the child in question was an adult now, so the privacy laws didn't apply so much anymore. He was hoping he could get a local judge in the small beach town to agree to let him have access to the records. Maybe a name or another kid in foster care would remember her.

"Send me everything you've got, and I'll figure out if I

can file a request with the court for more. Also, if you have the grandmother's previous address before she ended up in the nursing home, maybe a neighbor remembers her."

The investigator agreed and said he was sending Finn everything he had on the case. Finn bypassed going home and went straight into the office, eager to draft the inheritance documents Maddox requested and then review the files from the PI. An hour later, he heard the elevator doors open.

Hailey! He tried to school his instant excitement. She wouldn't welcome a big display of attention. She wore simple black slacks and a gray blouse that set off her aquamarine eyes. Her pert pink lips spread in a huge smile, and she stopped just inside his office. He stood.

"Oh, hey, I didn't expect anyone else to be here today," he said with exaggerated surprise and looked around as if someone might overhear them.

"Very funny. There's no one else here to see your terrible acting."

"Bummer."

She pulled a muffin from her purse and set it on his desk.

"Thank you," he whispered.

"Did you get your other casework done?"

"No, but I can put it off if you want to work on our joint case now." He itched to reach out and touch her, but it would be a mistake. He had to respect her need for boundaries.

She looked at her watch. "I need to get my bearings and review everything. Let's meet in about an hour in the conference room."

"See you there." He turned away and sat back down at his desk before he grabbed her and kissed her.

The next hour was a struggle to concentrate, knowing Hailey's gorgeous body was only ten feet away. He completed the paperwork he needed to request the old documents and then read through every file the investigator had sent over. Virginia Beach was only two hours away from the city. He could go there and back in a day once this big case was done. He was familiar with that drive after having been posted to Virginia Beach as a SEAL.

Before he could delve into it, Hailey appeared in his doorway.

"Ready?" She glanced down to see the books he'd pulled from the law library.

"Inheritance law. Yikes, that sounds enthralling."

"More like mind-numbing." He grabbed his laptop, notebook, and locked his desktop computer. The firm's policy was to make sure no one could read the files you were working on because there was always so much client personal information in their files.

They made their way up the elevator into the conference room, keeping a safe distance and not touching once. It was brutal. Purposefully, he sat across from her in the conference room and fought every urge to reach for her, lay her on the table, and explore her body with his mouth.

"Tomorrow in court, I think you should take the lead. The defense will try to overpower me, embarrass me with talk about adult toys, and sexual preferences. You can counter that by taking the lead, present the law, and gloss over their attempt to make this about a rich man and poor wife. This was a business Mrs. Tovar created on her own and in spite of her wealthy, stingy husband," Hailey said with conviction.

"Respectfully, I disagree. You should take point because they will look like children when they try to embarrass you. We'll use their biases against them from the start."

She started to argue, but he held up his hand. "Hear me out? Mrs. Tovar hid her business to shield herself and her son from the explicit nature of the toys and people's judgment. But as you so eloquently said, women do not need to be ashamed of their bodies, their desires, their needs. They can take care of themselves. Mrs. Tovar has embodied that by going out on her own. You do not blush easily, and you're too stubborn to let them intimidate you with a few sex toys."

Hailey grinned as she considered his argument.

"Mrs. Tovar did say she specifically wanted something for herself when it became clear her husband wasn't a real partner in life. He used his money to control her and their family. The business based around pleasure toys for women was her way of taking back control while also saying he wasn't enough, he wasn't god's gift to her, she wasn't going to just take what he gave her."

"Bingo. So you lead, and we go with the angle that Mrs. Tovar was never ashamed of her needs not being met, not then or now. She was methodical, smart, and took care of it on her own."

"What if Mrs. Tovar balks at this?"

"You prep her. She believes in you."

"Us."

"It will resonate better coming from you, woman to woman."

She nodded. The client coaching for court could often be the most difficult part of a case. People reacted emotionally when their character was being attacked in court, it was difficult to separate the theatrics of it, and if they were too good at ignoring it, they looked cold and guilty.

"Let's practice. I'll pretend to be the cocky male defense lawyer, and you be your polished, poised, kick-butt self," Finn said, standing from the table.

"How do you know they won't also use a woman in their defense?"

"We don't. It's just a hunch. Mr. Tovar is a weak man who needs to exert his wealth as his power. He never viewed his wife as an equal—she was an accessory to his life. I don't think he'd want a female attorney to solve his problem for him. Also, there were only men listed on their firm's website."

Hailey laughed, and he enjoyed the sound as it rolled over him. "Good attention to detail. Do you think most men view their wives as partners?"

He studied her. She hadn't experienced any great examples of healthy relationships growing up. It was the complete opposite for Finn.

"Any real man would expect his wife to be a partner, I would think, based on all the examples in my family. And come to think of it, my mom probably just lets my dad think he has half a say, so maybe the imbalance is skewed in favor of the women. Both my brothers and brother-in-law are fools for their wives. I can't see them getting away with trying to boss their wives around." He laughed at the thought.

She fidgeted but didn't meet his eyes. He took a step closer.

"In all seriousness, a woman should expect to be viewed as an equal in a relationship. Her needs, wants, desires should all matter. And if a man loves her, all her needs will matter more than his own. People should always put their loved ones first."

"That sounds like a nice sentiment, but I wonder how many people find that kind of love?"

"Well, it exists, so why settle for less?" he asked.

The tension between them was palpable. If Hailey could let down her guard long enough, he would cherish her and put all her needs before his. He'd never wanted to be tied to someone more than in that moment.

"Okay, so let's get started." She turned away and cleared her throat.

✕

THEY SPENT THE next hour sparring and rehearsing different arguments and tactics the defense could use in court. Finn pushed her with more aggressive verbal judo than he'd expect from any respectable attorney, but he doubted Mr. Tovar hired them for their courtside manner. Hailey rose to the occasion and met him every step of the way, with precise, calm rebuttals or redirection. She was exceptional.

"You're ready, Hailey. We're ready to win this case."

"Don't get overconfident. They may have a few more tricks up their sleeves."

"Speaking of, you know who else might have some great insights before we head into court tomorrow?"

She looked at him suspiciously.

"Judge Cora Maguire, who happens to be hosting a dinner tonight, and you're invited."

A smile split her face. "Sunday family dinner?"

He took one step closer, careful not to touch her.

"Yes, I want you to come with me as my date, not my colleague. But it doesn't hurt that my mom would love to talk strategy and law with you."

Biting her lip, she narrowed her eyes. "Okay, you twisted my arm. Do you need to work more, or are you ready?" She took a half step closer, stopping only an inch away from his chest. "If we leave now, we could stop by your place and freshen up," she said.

It was clear she wanted to get dirty with him, thus the reason to clean up—and he was one hundred percent on board.

He dropped his voice into a low whisper and leaned toward her ear. "As soon as we leave this building, I'm going to give you what you want."

Her breath caught and she gripped his shirt, but in the next moment, she pushed away from him and grabbed her laptop before stomping toward the door.

"Last one to the car is on top," she called out.

"Is that a threat or a promise?" he hollered to her back as he collected his notes. Quickly, he shuffled his things into his bag and locked up the conference room. She'd already gone down in the elevator, likely to grab her bag and beat him to the car, but he used the stairs. When he popped into the third floor, he was surprised to see Smith at the end of the rookie hallway, towering over Hailey, who was being backed into a corner.

"Why were you snooping around in my office, Smith. What were you looking for?"

Her words barely registered before Smith moved closer and Finn saw red, but before he could do anything, Hailey's hand struck out to strike Smith's throat.

Gasping for breath, Smith staggered backward.

Finn gripped his shoulder to make his presence known and Smith tried to pull away, but Finn held his upper arm as Hailey skirted past him into her office.

"Hey, you get something stuck in your throat, Smith?" Finn asked, as he applied pressure to let him know he better back off.

"Not quite. He was rifling through my desk," Hailey said.

Smith finally caught his breath.

"Look, man, I was just looking for the keys to the library. She's always forgetting to return them to the communal drawer. Then she attacked me."

"I have my own set. You were looking for something, and I want to know what," she accused, stepping closer, but Finn put up his forearm to stop her. Their colleague was definitely lying. Smith wasn't even trying to mask his dislike for Hailey today.

"Little ice princess, I see you've used your assets to get Finn to do your bidding too."

"Easy, Smith. What were you doing here? You never come in on weekends."

A sneer spread on Smith's face as he looked from Hailey to Finn.

"You're on the wrong team, Maguire. She's not going to sleep with you, and even if she does, it's not going to gain you any favor if she makes partner."

Finn stepped in front of Hailey to block the ugliness Smith was spewing. "Time for you to go."

Smith's sneer turned into a devious smile. "When you two lose this case, neither of you will make partner."

"What makes you think we could lose?" Hailey challenged, stepping from behind Finn. But Smith just chuckled and picked up his hat off the floor where it must have fallen earlier when Hailey struck him.

He felt like he was in a haze of red-hot anger and turned to Hailey.

"Did he touch you?" he asked, trying not to direct his annoyance at her.

"No." She stomped into her office. "He was going to regret it if he did, but you arrived before that happened."

Moving stiffly, he walked into her office and closed the door behind him.

"Hailey," he said with a forced calm he didn't at all feel.

Finally, she paused her search of her office for anything out of place and met his eyes.

"I don't have any right to tell you what to do, I know that. But please don't let anyone ever back you into a corner like that again. It puts you at an automatic disadvantage."

"I can defend myself, but you're right. You don't have the right to tell me what to do."

Finn's shoulders stiffened, and he took a deep breath.

"I know I don't, but when I saw him closing in on you, I felt the two worst emotions: fear and panic."

"Like him, you have no idea what I'm capable of but I will never let anyone get the upper hand on me again. He wasn't ever going to keep me cornered."

"Babe."

"Not here." With one last look around her office, she opened the door and waited for him to exit. "Smith was up to something shady snooping through my office, and I need to know what."

Finn's adrenaline crashed. He'd wanted to rip Smith's smirk off his face, and now he'd like to tuck Hailey away in a hidden posh tower, where no one could ever hurt her again.

When he didn't move, she stopped in front of him and studied him. Moments ticked by until she lifted one hand up to caress his face. She ran her delicate, cool fingers over his frown and the lines of his forehead.

"I'll be more careful," she conceded. "I promise he was one step away from my knee in his groin and a bloody nose from the palm of my hand in his face." She gently looped her hands behind his neck and stood on her tiptoes to place a light kiss on his lips.

Before she could say any more, he took over the kiss. He needed to feel closer to her and know she was safe and still his. He needed to brand her with his mouth, even if no one could see it or know she belonged to him. Pulling her back into her office, he closed the door and locked it again, then pushed her up against the edge of her desk. She sat and spread her legs, making room for him to stand between her thighs. Her mouth and hands were just as needy as he felt.

When she began to undo his belt buckle, he couldn't fight the smile that pulled at his lips.

"Damn you, Finn Maguire, with your sexy, heroic need to protect me and this lush mouth. You force me to cross my own lines."

A laugh escaped him. "You should talk, luring me in for the slaughter with your soft skin, brilliant mind, and dirty talk." He unbuttoned her blouse to reveal her perky breasts covered by a thin camisole.

Laughing, she teased him between kisses while helping him lift his shirt off then doing the same with hers. "Nothing like armbars and finance law to get you going, baby."

Her voice was deeper from the lust coursing between them, and he didn't miss the term of endearment she let slip. Running his hands over her delicate skin he watched as goosebumps rose up along his path. With one hand he ran his thumb over the pebbled peak beneath the thin material of her bra and leaned forward to kiss her neck before moving down her chest, causing her breath to hitch.

"You're mine," he said with distinction as he cupped the back of her head with both hands, and his thumbs framed her face.

She met his eyes, searching for something.

"And no one is ever going to hurt you."

She nodded before he sealed his promise with more kisses and then lay her back on the desk to trail his mouth down to her waist.

"You're not going to regret this," he said as he unbuttoned her dress pants.

"I already don't, not one bit," she said.

He ran his hands down her legs, pushing her pants to the floor, then back up her thighs as he kneeled in front of her spread out on the desk. She was offering herself up to him and he was going to give as good as he got. Hopefully, she could feel the shift in his desire for her. It transcended physical need—he wanted her mind, body, and heart.

Chapter Fourteen

Hailey

TWO HOURS LATER Hailey had trouble wiping off the smile Finn put on her face. After being thoroughly unprofessional in her office, he took her back to his home where he proceeded to worship her body more. The man was a sex god, but it was more emotional than basic orgasmic bliss. Something behind his kisses and caresses made her feel like she was the only woman in the world he could ever need. There was no other way to describe his attention to every inch of her body. He gave her tender kisses, nips with his teeth, and sinful licks of her skin until she was a ball of confused emotions but satisfactorily spent.

She enjoyed being in his home, among his things, but was surprised it didn't seem more homey or lived in, like he wasn't settled in his life. His condo had high ceilings with big windows to let in light and reveal amazing views of the river cutting between Virginia and Washington D.C. Wide plank, light oak wood floors that felt heated under her feet were accented by stylish home furnishings. A modern white-and-gray kitchen commanded one wall, and it was comfortable but also didn't give clues about the man that lived there.

His bedroom was a soothing shade of blue with cozy lush bedding, but there were no personal knickknacks or pictures. There was only one item that caught her eye.

"Is that my scarf on your dresser?" she asked, lounging in his arms in bed.

"Yes."

"Were you going to give it back to me?"

"Probably when it lost your scent," he said.

Smiling, she turned back to face him and found his serious bright green eyes watching how she would react to his confession. She crawled over him to rest her chin on his chest.

"You like me," she said.

"I like you very much."

"You can keep the scarf," she said.

If she was going to have to give him up, she wanted to enjoy all the time with him now.

"Why does your home look like it's only a temporary situation?"

He took a deep breath.

"I've only had this place a few years, and to be honest, it doesn't really feel like home. I guess it does feel temporary. When I retired my commission with the Navy I took some time off and stayed with my folks." He laughed. "I know that seems odd for a twenty-something-year-old SEAL to stay with his parents, but I just needed time to rest and recoup."

"That makes perfect sense, especially with your folks. Heck, I'd like to go be spoiled at your parents' house for a week or two."

His hand was stroking her back, and his smile told her he understood how fortunate he was to have the kind of parents he has.

"Once I got into law school, I got this place. It's comfortable and in a great location, but I guess I still think of my folks' place as home."

"You were probably so used to moving from place to place you didn't know how to create a permanent home."

"Hmmm, yah, I guess I'll just keep borrowing your things and fill this place up until it seems more homey," he said, rolling her on her back and kissing her eyes.

"Not a terrible idea. I've probably maxed out the number of books and plants at my house. Now that I know I'm sleeping with a thief, I can start populating my place with extra things for you to take."

"Or just move in here and save me the trouble," he said matter-of-factly.

"What?" Her eyes popped open.

"Don't freak out. It just came out, but now that I think about it, that could work. You said you're outgrowing your place. Mine is bigger with better safety features: doorman, secure garage, live-in boyfriend trained to kill. It's a logical idea."

She suddenly felt confined under his body in his huge bed and pushed up on her elbow.

"Boyfriend?"

"Yes, a regular male companion with whom one has a romantic relationship. I looked it up because I knew you'd freak."

"I can't just move in."

Rolling off her onto his side, he placed one hand under his head. A playful smirk spread on his face.

"Okay, Miss Independent, why can't you move in? Clearly, we are very well suited. Our connection is like a raging fire that I doubt will ever go out, much less dwindle, anytime soon. We like the same food, both practice law, and oh, I'm obsessed with your body."

"Moving in with someone is a huge step; it's like a precursor to being married. People move in together to test the waters and make sure they don't drive each other insane."

"Okay."

Flipping back the covers, she stood from the bed and picked up the first piece of clothing she could find, which happened to be his T-shirt. It draped over her body to hang at her mid-thigh and only enticed him to try to peek under it while his hands reached out to her. Instead of responding to him, she started to gather her things.

"Is this your mature way of telling me you're not ready to think of our relationship like that, that you don't see a possible future with me?" Finn asked.

She stopped in her tracks, faced him, and gave a huge sigh.

"I haven't thought about it. I don't think ahead like that with people."

"But you've planned out your future career wise—why not consider if there is someone—me—by your side in that future, cheering you on?"

Her mouth opened and closed like a fish, until finally, she found her voice. "Up until this moment, I thought this thing between us was just a fling or maybe your attempt to keep me distracted so you could win this case and get the junior partner position."

"Now that's bullshit. I've been very clear about my attraction and feelings for you. Just because you want to pretend not to notice I'm falling for you doesn't mean I'm some dirtbag trying to steal a partnership we both know you've earned."

Finn sat up now in bed and propped himself up with pillows. The sheets fell to rest below his six-pack of abs, and she had a hard time getting annoyed with him looking so deliciously enticing in bed.

"I don't know how far a person will go to manipulate me or try to take what I want," she said in her defense.

Finn took a deep inhale and crossed his arms over his chest, causing his muscles to ripple and flex, but a smile played on his mouth.

"Okay, I accept that. But just so we are one hundred percent clear, Hailey Adams, I am enthralled and impressed by your mind and work ethic. Your passion for the law is inspiring. I believe the partners have already made their decision but wanted you to tap into the idea that you won't always have to win every case or do everything on your own. Making partner will mean you have a dozen colleagues that have your back and will help you win, not just because they have financial incentives for the firm to succeed, but because you'll be part of that team."

"I never thought of it like that."

"Babe, I understand you have had to fight and scrounge for everything, and you have been conditioned to expect the worst of people. I understand it's not professional for me to have fallen for you while we're working on a very important case, but I need you to know this was never about winning the case. For me, it was always about winning you. I know moving in together is a big step and probably a while away. But we are in a relationship, and when you're ready to discuss it, I would like to talk about a future unrelated to where either of us work."

"Tomorrow is a really big day for us, and I need to get a good night's sleep," she said.

Finn's exhale said it all. He was disappointed she was taking the easy way out, but she wasn't ready to make any big decisions about them. There was still the possibility that their relationship would end once one of them was selected for partner. She wasn't as confident as him that the firm already planned to select her.

He held back the covers. His invitation was clear.

"Come back to bed, and I promise I won't keep you up all night."

"No, you have dinner with your parents, and I need to go home and get my mind right for tomorrow."

Folding himself out of the sheets, he walked around the bed to stand in front of her, naked.

"Okay, let me get a quick shower, and I'll take you home on my way to my folks."

A sudden wave of her deep need for independence was crashing into her desire to be with Finn and let him be there for her. His little thoughtful habits all combined to prove that he was always looking out for her. It was nice, but not something she should let herself get used to if things weren't going to last.

"Actually, I think I'd like to just head home now. I'll get the bus."

"On a Sunday evening, it'd take forever." He grabbed his jeans off the floor and put them on. "I'll take you now if you're in a hurry and then come back to get ready, no big deal."

She huffed. "Why are you being so nice to me when I'm trying to keep you at arm's length?"

His laugh only made it more difficult.

"Because I understand it. I'm not mad. If you need more time to fall for my charms, then I'll give you more time."

"These Jedi mind tricks make me second-guess myself."

With his strong arms, he enveloped her in a big hug, and she couldn't resist hugging him back.

"No tricks, baby. I'm just here when you're ready, once you work this all out in your beautiful mind."

"I really do need to get home and make sure I'm ready for tomorrow," she said as they swayed, their bodies still melded in a tight hug.

"I understand. But you have to put some pants on before I'll let you leave my place, and I would consider it a big favor if you let me just take you home."

She nodded, unable to fight his need to know she's home safe. It was luxurious to have someone worry about her, and she couldn't resist it. Once she was dressed in her own clothes, she let Finn hold her hand while they made their way back down to the garage. He opened her car door and drove her home, where he also got out of the car, opened her car door, and walked her to her doorstep.

"Don't stay up all night worrying. We're ready for tomorrow, and you will win this case," he said with fierce conviction.

"Thank you for understanding."

With a long, sensuous kiss, Finn imprinted himself further on her heart, something she thought had stopped working when her grandmother died.

"I'll see you in the morning," he promised before she let herself in her apartment then watched his car pull away.

Move in with him.

They'd worked together for years but only got to really know each other over the last few weeks. How could he be so sure she wouldn't drive him nuts or he wouldn't get sick of her in a few more weeks? What made him think he'd even still like her next week?

The questions, instead of the biggest case of her career, plagued her well into the night.

✕

THE NEXT DAY, Hailey couldn't shake the feeling that something would go wrong in court. She arrived bright and early to ensure they had their case on the docket, and she knew which courtroom they would be in. She also managed to reserve a lawyer's box for them, which was just a small room where clients could speak with the lawyers and witnesses could be staged while waiting to address the court. Dread filled her when she spotted Smith arrive at the courthouse. He was with another man who looked at least ten years older, wore an expensive suit, and had an even more smug look.

It made no sense for Smith to be here today. He didn't have any cases in court. As a first-year rookie, he wasn't entrusted to represent the firm in court alone yet, and at the rate he was going, she doubted he ever would progress. Smith caught her watching him and glared before heading into the courtroom. The same courtroom where her case was being tried.

"Morning. Was that Smith?" Finn asked with a gentle nudge to her elbow.

"Yes, and I think it's safe to assume he's not on our side."

Before they could dwell on it, Mrs. Tovar arrived. Hailey ushered them into their client room. Most days the judge was on time but their case wasn't the first one that morning and they could use the time to give their client a final pep talk.

"I'm really nervous, but I keep telling myself this is my business and I don't need my ex's permission to keep it," Mrs. Tovar said.

"Remember, we're expecting them to try to embarrass us, shame us, and try some desperate trick because they have no case. No proof that your ex has any legal claim to your business," Hailey coached. "Don't cringe, don't hang your head, don't react no matter what they say."

"At this point, I'm all in, and you were right about my son. He said he wasn't embarrassed about my work at all. He said he was proud of me." She beamed.

The phone rang, and it was time to head to court.

Everything went as expected in the first twenty minutes. The judge blocked Mr. Tovar's attempt to sell a company he didn't own. Next, his attorneys attempted to make the judge and Hailey blush by talking about the types of products Pleasure Inc produced. They hammered home the assessment that the company was geared toward giving women pleasure.

"With all due respect, Your Honor, as my client has been the mastermind behind development, sales, and promotion of every single product, we are well aware of what Pleasure Inc has to offer. I think we can all agree, this company is a sophisticated adult pleasure toy manufacturer and supplier geared toward women," Hailey said, looking from the judge to the plaintiff's slick lawyer.

His polished demeanor flinched.

"Indeed we can, Ms. Adams."

Having the judge rule again in her favor was sure to make the plaintiff and his attorneys more hostile, but the lead attorney painted on a smarmy grin.

"Before you attempt a rebuttal and request an example of what pleasure is, Counselor, let's all also agree we understand this business up for dispute is just that. A successful and lucrative business, full stop," the judge said.

Hailey couldn't help but smile.

"Your Honor, of course we agree. Our point being in order to develop such a broad range of pleasure toys"—he let his eyes scan Hailey's suit-clad figure up and down—"the owner of the company would need to conduct market research, testing, and toy development."

The judge nodded. "And your point is?"

The lawyer held up a stack of papers before dropping one set on the table in front of Hailey and handing one to the bailiff, who delivered it to the judge.

"We would like to submit new evidence that proves Mr. Tovar was involved in the selection of researchers based on this email exchange."

Hailey skimmed the first page before setting it back down.

"Your Honor, the plaintiff has had our robust request for discovery for weeks. This last-minute parlor trick to submit new evidence on day one is a stall tactic."

"Counselors, approach the bench," the judge requested.

"Your Honor, we only discovered these emails yesterday that prove Mr. Tovar was the decision-maker for this lucrative business."

Alarms went off in Hailey's mind. Had she left something out for Smith to find in her office? Did he somehow have access to her emails with Mrs. Tovar?

"Who is the email exchange with? You'll need to prove relevance before I let you submit them," the judge said.

"The emails are from Mrs. Tovar's personal email and involve a research contractor named Billie Monroe."

The hairs went up on the back of Hailey's neck. She knew that name but couldn't be sure how.

"Your Honor, my client never volunteered her personal email account for review, and there was no warrant served to retrieve this."

"It wasn't necessary," the plaintiff's attorney said. "Your client's email was stored on the joint family cloud, and in this instance, as you will see, she forwarded her emails to Mr. Tovar, giving him permission to access."

"It does appear these were forwarded, Ms. Adams. But I'll give you a day to review them and determine what to make of them. We'll reconvene tomorrow afternoon," the judge announced.

With a smile, Hailey returned to her side of the courtroom. The judge made her ruling, and they were all dismissed.

"Do not let them goad you," Hailey said under her breath to Finn next to her. She stepped away to whisper the same thing in Mrs. Tovar's ear but in a nicer tone.

"We'll reconvene at the firm. Don't let them see you sweat. This is their desperate last attempt."

Mrs. Tovar smiled and met Hailey's eyes. "Sophisticated pleasure toys?"

Hailey fought a grin. "Well, when you add sophisticated to anything, it makes it sound high end."

"I'm going to add that slogan to our PR campaign," Mrs. Tovar said.

"Good luck trying to steal from me now, Sara," Mr. Tovar barked over the aisle between their opposing sides of the court. "You won't get a dime from me, and our son will be coming to live with me full-time."

"Get your client under control," Finn said with such authority a chill ran down Hailey's back.

The bailiffs also keyed in on the commotion and stepped in, moving Mr. Tovar and his gaggle of lawyers toward the exit. Smith smirked at Hailey before he followed them out.

Finn placed his hand on the small of her back. "I recommend we exit via the garage where I parked. There was already press when we arrived."

"How did you park in the courthouse garage?" Hailey asked.

"Perks of being a Maguire." He grinned unabashedly.

"I have a car service waiting," Mrs. Tovar said.

"It's highly likely your ex-husband is out front making some bombastic claims about winning in court today. We don't want to add fuel to the flame," Hailey said.

"I want to read these emails," Mrs. Tovar said.

"Let's take Finn's car and wait to discuss anything until we're back at the firm."

Mrs. Tovar agreed. "Is it weird I actually enjoyed watching you run circles around his lawyers? I'm looking forward to tomorrow," Mrs. Tovar said with a grin and followed Finn to the exit.

Hailey let out a deep breath. One more day, and she'd finally finish this case.

A half hour and one odd car ride later, with a stop for cupcakes per Mrs. Tovar's request, they were all seated in the conference room. Hailey pulled out the stack of emails while Finn and Mrs. Tovar indulged in the decadent cupcakes.

"Before we get started on these emails, we need to know how often, if at all, you included your husband in your business dealings."

"Absolutely never. This is a conflation of the truth. These emails aren't me asking for permission to work with Ms. Monroe. I was telling him to stay out of my business. Do you know who Billie Monroe is?"

"No," they replied.

"She was the famous D.C. madam they tried to nail on tax evasion a few years ago, but it didn't stick because she's too smart. Her girls never offer anything beyond companionship, and she has several high-end lawyers in her pocket. But she's an expert on meeting people's needs, and I hired her as a consultant."

"Wow," Hailey said, genuinely surprised.

"Thank you. Not bad for an unsuspecting housewife whose husband ignored her. About six months ago, Billie told me there was a conflict of interest because my husband was trying to solicit her services. She asked me to get him to stop bothering her."

"Those emails were my first attempt to let him know I was aware of his extramarital activities. He wasn't embarrassed, only pissed that I'd ruined his ability to hire the most sought-after service in town."

Finn was reading through the emails, and his head popped up. "She's right, but why would they claim it was more? This exchange proves nothing."

"Perception can be anything you tell a person. It doesn't have to be true and the people don't even have to really believe it. Once it's out there, it's real. Mr. Tovar has been telling the press for weeks this is his business. We're missing something. They must have needed more time for something," Hailey said.

"It must be why Smith was snooping around our offices and was in court today," Finn said.

Hailey began to pace. "Mrs. Tovar, when we first met, you said you weren't going to let your husband get credit for your inventions and take your company. So you filed for divorce, and he countered with a lawsuit for Pleasure Inc." They hadn't even discussed her patents for her very lucrative business.

"Correct." Mrs. Tovar stood and began to pace making it

clear she was uneasy with the fact that her two high-paid lawyers still didn't know what her ex was up to.

"Forgive me, but the sex toy industry seems to have been pretty well covered. What invention is left?"

Mrs. Tovar smirked. "Well, you are partially right, but something that came up a lot in my market research was the concept of an AI feature. A toy that could read a woman's physical needs and react with a pleasurable response to her body."

"You invented a smart sex toy?" Finn asked, impressed.

"Billie and I did, but she was worried my ex would try to insert himself in this."

"Did you get the patent already?" Hailey asked.

"We filed it the day I filed for divorce."

"Well done," Hailey said.

"I bet they thought it was in the personal items they seized in her office, and assumed they overlooked it," Finn said. "We need to make sure your partner won't get cold feet or be intimidated by Mr. Tovar and his lawyers."

"Oh, she won't, but she'll probably play with them for a bit before she tells them to piss off. That woman really does enjoy screwing with men."

"Good, then we're ready for court tomorrow—they expected us to have this wrapped up today," Finn said.

×

THE NEXT DAY in court, the judge had enough of Mr. Tovar's stall tactics. Haily and Finn had Ms. Monroe appear in court to testify she and Mrs. Tovar were business partners and Mr. Tovar had no place in their work. The judge ruled in Mrs. Tovar's favor on all counts. The divorce was granted, primary custody was granted to Mrs. Tovar, and the judge found no evidence that Pleasure Inc was funded at all by Mr. Tovar. Mrs. Tovar was vindicated, and Hailey and Finn had won.

Back at the office, they found out Smith had already quit and cleared out his desk.

Now all that remained was for the partners to select their new junior partner. Suddenly, Hailey wasn't ready to know, because either way, it meant things with Finn would have to end. But at the same time, this was what she had been waiting for, and she needed to know if all those years of hard work were going to pay off.

"So how are you two going to celebrate this win?" Mr. Baxter asked as they sat next to each other at the conference room table in the partners' suite.

"Actually, I was thinking of taking a few days off," Finn said. "I have a lead on the other case I've been working on, and it requires a little road trip."

Mr. Baxter nodded.

"I think that is a fantastic idea. Why don't you both take a few days off? Hailey, I don't think you've taken a single day of leave in the four years you've worked here," Mrs. Stewart said.

"Done, we don't want to see either of you in the office until Friday. In the meantime, the managing partners will deliberate on our decision for this year's junior partner," Baxter said and stood to end the meeting.

"Sir, I have other cases to work on, too, and Finn just

said he'd be working."

"Hailey, your dedication is commendable, but everyone deserves a little downtime. I can't force you not to work from home, but don't let me see you in the office until Friday." Then he left the conference room, and Mrs. Stewart gave her a wink before she departed too.

"Looks like you're free to go with me tomorrow, unless you've got plans to pout and be upset with me for getting us a few days off," Finn said with a big grin.

She wanted to be pissed, but his adorable and sexy smirk was impossible to resist.

"You're incorrigible."

"Is that a yes?"

"I'm not sure."

"What's the hesitation?"

"I'm just worried about what happens next," she said with more honesty than she planned.

"Come with me on this road trip and pretend there is nothing to worry about."

His tone was carefree and inviting, but she knew the more time they spent together, the harder it would be when it ended. "Let me see how much I can accomplish today on my other caseload and think about it," she said as she headed to the door. If she didn't get some distance between them, she was going to end up kissing him in the managing partners' conference room.

"We leave at seven a.m. tomorrow, so you should probably just stay at my house," he whispered as he followed her into the empty elevator and pressed the number for their floor.

Her willpower disappeared once the doors closed.

"You can come to my house, and we'll leave from there," she decided.

"Deal."

His arm brushed hers, and his scent wafted around her.

Closing her eyes, she held her breath, fighting every urge to push the alarm again and stay locked in their own bubble.

Finn Maguire was forcing her to need him, and it was terrifying.

Chapter Fifteen

Finn

FINN COULDN'T FOCUS while the clock slowly ticked down to five o'clock. Which meant nothing, because Hailey never left on time. But five minutes after five, she texted him that she was leaving, and he nearly dropped his fresh coffee in his lap.

Wait for me, and I'll drive you, he fired back.

No thank you. I have a stop to make, but you can come over when you're ready.

I'm ready now!!!!

Smiley face blush emoji.

The simple, playful symbol was a way to say she was letting down her defenses. Hailey was like a beautiful princess hiding behind spiked walls she built, but he was fighting his way to her heart.

Don't you need to pack a bag?

No, I packed what I'll need this morning.

Cocky and presumptuous.

I prefer charming and irresistible.

More like shameless. I'll be home by six. See you then.

Before he could respond, she walked by his office with her bag but didn't say a word to anyone. Fighting the urge to shut down his computer, instead he opened up his files on the Admiral Maddox case. His trip to Virginia Beach was a bit of a wild goose chase, but he wanted to cover all his bases. His plan was to knock on the doors of the maternal grandmother's neighbors' houses and visit the senior care center where she spent her final days. He'd considered trying to bribe someone at the center to give him the name of the next of kin or a copy of the file. A huge inheritance was waiting in the wings for some poor kid who'd had a bad run of luck. But he couldn't risk his bar license over it.

Packing up his notes and his laptop, he managed to kill another twenty minutes, and decided to get flowers for Hailey on his way there.

With a bouquet of pink daisies and roses in hand, Finn buzzed the intercom outside Hailey's building.

"Come on up." Her voice cracked through the small metal box, and the door clicked to let him up.

With eager strides, he took the steps two at a time. She met him at the top step with her door open. He held up the flowers, and she rewarded him with a grin that made her eyes sparkle like stars in a deep blue sky. He dropped his bag and enveloped her with his free hand and placed several kisses on her neck before finding her lips.

"Mmm. Yep. You taste amazing," Finn said.

"You're in a good mood. Still riding the high on our big win?" she asked.

"No, I'm excited for a few days off with you."

She accepted the flowers, and he set his bag by the door, kicked off his shoes, and took in her tidy, cozy apartment.

The parquet wood floors shined. A large white couch

commanded the open space with a geometric gray-and-white rug under a simple ottoman. One wall was painted a soothing shade of blue. Another wall held colorful prints, and there was a fat orange tabby cat curled in a ball in a pet bed that looked like a smaller version of her couch.

Bookshelves filled to the brim lined the wall behind the couch. Beyond that was a small alcove with a table and an open kitchen. At the back of the apartment was a patio big enough for two chairs and it looked out over the alleyway and a park behind her building. Hailey stood watching him.

"I should have known your home would be cozy and inviting, just like you behind your tough exterior," Finn said, wrapping one arm around her and kissing her neck again.

"I don't think anyone else would describe me that way," Hailey said.

"Good, I don't need any competition for your attention." Nodding toward the cat, he said, "I didn't peg you for a cat person."

Hailey shrugged, and her cheeks were flushed, highlighting more cracks in her facade.

"So you come home after a long day to your cozy home, snuggle your cat, and think to yourself, *I wonder what Finn is doing*?" he teased.

A burst of laughter escaped her lips, but her blush grew even brighter red and her eyes twinkled.

"I guess I did wonder about you sometimes," she admitted. "Why were you so serious and never as childish as the other junior lawyers in the bullpen? You never seemed to let them tempt you to go out."

"I went out for a drink once or twice, but only long

enough to determine I'm too old for their idea of fun."

"Old souls." She stood in the open kitchen, putting the flowers in a water pitcher to serve as a vase.

The cat woke up and tilted his head to study Finn before stretching from his bed. Crouching down, Finn waited for the cat to smell him and decide if it would let him pet him. The blue collar had a tag with the name Tiger stamped on it.

Scooping the cat up, he gave it a good scratch, and it purred before licking his chin. Moving farther into the room, he scanned the old law books and decorative knickknacks. There were no photos, and the idea of Hailey having zero family or fond memories of childhood was like a punch to his gut. He couldn't imagine how lonely that would feel.

"How did you decide on law school?" he asked when she joined him in the living room.

She placed the flowers on the end table next to the couch and smiled.

"Oh, you know, a scrappy kid neglected by the system picks herself up by her bootstraps and goes to law school with a plan to right all the wrongs."

He let Tiger go and accepted the beer she offered him. The tang of a smooth local IPA gave him more insights into her tastes.

"Once I made it through my first year of law school and accepted some serious student loans, I decided I didn't want to be a broke public defender. So I set my sights on corporate law. I did a few pro bono internships and worked as a legal assistant at the local DA's office. My mentor was a law instructor and working lawyer who went to school with Inez Stewart. She said if I wanted to go private practice, I should work for Inez where I wouldn't have to sell my soul."

He sat in one corner of her couch enjoying the intimacy of being with her in her space and hearing her background.

"So Inez hired you?"

"No," she said. "If I wanted to practice corporate law, I needed to understand how corporations worked. She told me to get a job with a large company and learn every aspect of their business practices and then convince her I understood what rules they break and which they must abide by. So I did."

"When did you have time for school and working for a huge company?"

"My third year, I took a job with a major online distribution firm working nights. I learned everything I could about corporate holdings, management, and tax law. After I finished law school and passed the bar, Inez offered me a first-year position in the rookie bullpen."

"Damn, you're tougher than every SEAL I know."

She sipped her beer and shook off his compliment. "Some people have no choice but to be tenacious."

"That's not true. You could have just gotten a job. You didn't have to choose to go to school for seven years while working full-time and memorizing every aspect of law. Don't downplay your badassery."

Picking up her hand, he pulled her to sit next to him, and she didn't fight him. Instead, she burrowed into his side. They spent the next hour just talking. Once she started to fidget with the buttons on his shirt and started asking questions about the road trip they were taking, he could tell she was emotionally exhausted from sharing her background with him. Instead, he made love to her, pouring his admiration for her into every stroke of her delicate but fierce body. When they were both spent, she made him the best pasta dish he'd ever had before dragging him back into bed. With their naked bodies intertwined, she traced the lines of the eagle wing tattoo on his shoulder.

"Where are you going tomorrow?" she asked.

"We, you're coming with me," he pressed.

"I haven't decided," she said.

"There's a beach, so you'll need your bathing suit. I booked us a nice hotel. It even has one of those heart-shaped beds that vibrate when you feed it quarters." Her laugh echoed in the sparse room.

"Sounds so romantic, how could I resist?"

"It will be," he promised, flipping her on her back. He held her hands down on either side of her head, then he began licking his way down her body. "Please say you'll come with me, or I'll be too distracted to get back to your delicious body and I won't accomplish anything."

"Hmmm, so this is more about you?" She hummed. "What is this case about that it requires a road trip to a beach?"

"I can't tell you, client confidentiality. Very hush hush." He blew on her damp skin before placing more kisses along his path down her body and then traveling back up again.

"Intriguing."

Kissing her navel, he moved along her hip bones letting his scruff tickle her and enjoying her mewling reactions to him.

"Please, baby, come with me," he asked softly, letting his

breath flow over the epicenter between her legs as he slipped his palms under her bottom and squeezed her firm curves. He was going to enjoy convincing her as he sank his tongue down, licking the line where her leg met her pelvic bone. His mouth spread in a big smile when she yelled "yes" only a minute later.

The next morning, he let Hailey sleep while he showered, and he caught sight of one picture on the dresser in her room. It was tattered and in a small old brass frame. The young woman looked like Hailey but her hair was a light brown and her eyes were sad.

"If you're snooping, you won't find anything," Hailey said from bed.

"Was this your mother?"

"Yes. She was seventeen and hell-bent on growing up. I was born a year later." She sat up, and her blond hair fell around her shoulders.

"Do you keep in touch with your grandmother? I just assumed you didn't have any family."

"No, she died a few years ago."

"I'm sorry." He looked again at the young woman in the picture. What had happened to cause her to want to grow up so fast?

"They say it's a vicious cycle, having kids too young. My gran had my mom at eighteen, then my mom had me at eighteen."

"But you broke that cycle."

"I was terrified to have sex until I finished college."

"You were a virgin until after college?" he asked, sitting on the edge of the bed and facing her.

A sly smile curled up her mouth.

"Almost. At twenty, my senior year, I decided that being on the pill, using a condom, while tracking my most fertile time of the month, I could risk it."

"Rebel." He laughed. "I'm going to pretend you were a virgin until we met."

Now she laughed.

"I didn't see a coffee maker, why don't I go grab us some from the café downstairs while you get ready?"

Her eyes met his, and for a moment, he thought she would say she wasn't going. But instead, she kissed him then pulled back the sheets to stand in her naked glory before she walked toward the bathroom.

"Okay, but I could really use some help here first," she called out from the door, and he heard the shower turn on.

His shirt was off, and he shucked his jeans off in record time. When he stepped into the bathroom, she was bent over the sink with her hips pushed out and a wicked smile.

"We may as well get a little more dirty before we get cleaned up," he said.

Chapter Sixteen

Hailey

BEING WITH FINN was feeling more and more consuming. After a night and morning enjoying his attentive and healthy sex drive, she had trouble keeping her hands off him. He hadn't shaved, and a day's worth of scruff covered his square jaw outlining his lush lips. She swore his green eyes grew power from their kisses and nearly glowed right before he pushed her into orgasmic bliss. Not to mention his muscular form could make a paper bag look sexy. Right now, his carved thighs covered in jeans were spread to entice her as he sat in the driver's seat, and his forearms were taunting her to resist touching him. Maybe they could keep doing whatever this was if she got partner and he left the firm for JAG. It was two big ifs, but maybe it was a viable option.

"What is it?" he asked.

"You're sexy," she said.

His hand left the steering wheel and gripped her leg.

"Right back at you, but what were you really thinking?"

"I'm just taking it all in," she said, diverting her eyes to look out the window at the forest of trees along the highway. A sign read *Virginia Beach, 200 miles.*

"Are we going to a beach in Virginia?"

"Maybe, if you promise not to jump out of the car."

Her chest pounded, and all the feelings she pushed away the last time she was in Virginia Beach tumbled back to wash over her. She took a deep breath.

"Bad memories?"

"No, actually, just sad. That's where my gran lived."

"Oh, I'm sorry. I should have told you where I needed to go. I was worried you wouldn't want to sit in the car on such a long drive."

His hand enveloped hers, and she squeezed his back.

"No, it's fine. Actually, it would be nice to put some flowers on her grave. Who knows the next time I'll get back."

"Okay. I was planning to stop by the local city records office first. Then we can go wherever you want."

"Come to think of it, did you ever live in Virginia Beach?" she asked.

"I did when I first made the team, in between missions. But I was mostly on base, training or recovering."

"Huh, I wonder if we ever crossed paths and never knew it."

"I would remember you."

Her cheeks ached from smiling, but a sinking feeling began to form in her gut—how was she going to let him go? The idea of him leaving the firm had taken root in her mind, offering up a scenario for them to keep seeing each other—assuming she did make partner. But for now, she wasn't going to worry about it.

Once they arrived in Virginia Beach, Finn pulled onto

the main road along the coast, and they opened their windows to let the fresh salt air in.

"I'm not sure how long the courthouse will take," he said as he pulled into a parking lot outside the city clerk's office.

"I'm just along for the kisses," she blurted out. Something had shifted, and she couldn't seem to not be into this gorgeous attentive man.

"In that case..." He leaned over the center counsel to kiss her with such passion he stole her breath and had her debating on if they could fit in the back seat. "You'll have to wait until we get to the hotel," he said, squeezing her hip and. trailing kisses down her neck.

"Stop reading my mind."

Once out of the car, he held her hand as they walked into the old building and took a number to get in line and request records.

Not surprisingly, he had to fill out mounds of paperwork to request copies of old court documents and then wait for the clerk to find time to pull the files and make copies.

"What are you hoping to find in these documents anyway?" Hailey asked, unable to let her inquisitive mind stay dormant.

"Just old custody stuff." Finn waited in line again once he completed the forms and then turned with a grimace.

"Are you too hungry for one more stop?" he asked.

"Nope, I had snacks in my bag while you were filing paperwork so we can finish your work and then check into the hotel."

"You're so agreeable this close to the beach," he said, leading her back out to the car. Hugging her into his side, he wrapped one arm around her, and she slipped both arms around his waist to give him a tight squeeze.

"Truthfully, I'm just eager to check into our hotel and get you on that heart-shaped bed you mentioned," she said.

"Now you're talking."

Finn opened her door for her before they drove a few miles inland where the roads were all familiar. But when he pulled into a parking lot outside the rehab center and nursing home where her grandmother had stayed, her shoulders tightened, and the lightheartedness of the day washed away.

"Why are we here?" she asked with unease.

Finn turned off the car. "I think someone linked to my client died here. I know it's morbid, but I'm hoping they'll give me a copy of her file, and maybe the names of her next of kin."

Hailey realized dozens of elderly people probably died at the facility each year, but she didn't like the idea of walking back through the cold foyer or seeing the staff who look sad from dealing with sick or dying people all the time.

"I think I'll wait in the car, if that's okay?"

"Sure. If you'd rather, I can take you to the hotel first and come back."

"No, we're here. I'll just get some fresh air out by the pond while I wait." She pointed to a man-made pond off to the right with a few benches.

"Okay, you keep the keys in case you get hot."

Sitting on the stone bench, Hailey wondered who would hire a corporate lawyer to track down an old family member. Why wouldn't they do it themselves? People could be so cold and impersonal. Maybe it was a family member they never knew. She always assumed she must have some relatives on her dad's side she never met. Did they ever even know she existed?

"Well, that was a wasted stop. They said they destroy all the personal records a year after someone dies," Finn said as he strolled up.

"Sorry." She was relieved they could go.

"Hey, how'd you know about this pond?" he asked, rubbing his hand up her back and giving her neck a gentle squeeze.

"My gran lived here for a little bit, after a stroke. We tried rehab, and she seemed to be making some progress but then had another stroke and died."

Finn sat next to her and swooped her into his lap. "Why didn't you say anything? I'm sorry. This must be really shocking and sad to be here."

She fiddled with his shirt and thought about how she really was feeling being back in the town where she'd found a semblance of family.

"I didn't really know my grandmother all that well, but she did show me kindness. She helped me, and I helped her, until she got sick and died."

A tear slid down her face, and Finn gently swiped it away with his thumb before kissing her eyes. Hailey let herself feel the disappointment of losing the one link to her past, and the comfort Finn offered. Just like her grandmother, Finn accepted her for exactly who she was, scars and all. And he was alive and wanted her. Why shouldn't she keep him? Even if she didn't make partner, maybe he was reason enough to stay in Alexandria.

"Alright, let's get you back to the hotel. There's nothing like a hot shower and about a thousand kisses to make you feel a little better."

She laughed. "That does sound like a nice cure for the blues."

"I've got the remedy," he said, pulling her to a stand and hugging her on the walk back to the car.

As she buckled her seat belt, she felt oddly better telling Finn more about her past.

"Didn't you say you had two more stops? Where is the last one?" she asked.

"Nah, I'll go tomorrow while you rest in the morning." He started the car, and his hand enveloped hers, soothing her tattered emotions more than she ever realized she needed.

"Let's just go now, and then we can both relax more."

He looked at his watch. It was only eleven, and they both knew the hotel check-in wasn't until one.

"Are you sure?" he asked with a caution she didn't expect.

"Yes."

Ten minutes later, they were parked on a street she knew very well, because it was her grandmother's old street. They parked directly across from the small duplex she'd shared for a few years with her grandmother.

"Is the woman you're looking for named Cecilia Ray Burke?" she said through the tightness in her throat.

Finn turned toward her with surprise. "How did you know that?"

"She was my maternal grandmother. That was her house

with the blue shutters and flower boxes."

Finn shook his head. "Are you sure? I mean, of course you're sure. I'm just trying to figure this out. So when you ran away from foster care it was in North Carolina, you came here to stay with your maternal grandmother. And she died when you were in college."

"Yes, and I was so scared when I first arrived that the foster care system would catch up to me that I didn't go to school or get my GED until I turned eighteen. Soon after I started college, my grandmother had her first stroke and she had to stay at the senior home, but her house was paid for so I stayed here until she died. Eventually the state seized the property, but by then I was working and finishing up my bachelors at school an hour away. I managed to qualify for low budget student housing and never had a reason to come back here."

"And your last name is of course your dad's, not your mom's maiden name, Burke."

"Right."

"Who is looking for her and why?" Hailey asked, afraid to meet his eyes.

Finn cursed. "I can't say."

"Finn, you drag me on this wild goose chase and force me down memory lane because someone is paying a very high hourly rate, for you to track down the one relative to ever show me any love. And you won't tell me who or why they're looking for her?"

"I want to. I just owe it to the client to decide whether they want to tell you. I wouldn't want to get your hopes up."

"I can assure you I have no hopes for good news, and if

it's a debt collector, they can forget it. The state took all my gran's assets." Tears of frustration filled her eyes and trickled down her cheeks. Her stomach was in knots.

"Technically, you do work for the same firm, but I don't know if this is all real yet. The private investigator had that nursing home and this address listed for your grandmother, and she wrote the client a letter. But I don't understand why she never told you."

"Told me what?" Hailey said, dread was sour in her belly. Who would be looking for her grandmother, and how could it involve her? Unless it had something to do with her mother?

"Do you know something about my mother?"

"Screw it, I care more about you than my job at the firm. It's possible the man you thought was your father and abandoned you, wasn't actually your biological dad." He let out a breath he'd been holding while she processed what he was saying. "Admiral Maddox thinks he's your father, and he's been looking for you for years. Ever since your grandmother sent him a letter when you turned eighteen."

To say she was stunned was an understatement of grand proportions. Hailey knew enough about Maddox to know the man was a successful businessman with a penchant for technology and worth millions. There was no possible way he was her biological father.

"Why did my gran think I was related to Admiral Maddox?" she challenged.

"He said he knew your mother, they spent a summer together, but when he returned from a tour, she had married someone else. He assumed it had been a one-sided love affair and moved on. Then he received a letter from your grandmother detailing how your mom had been pregnant when she got married and included a baby picture of you. Maddox said he knew you were his." Finn gripped her hands that shook.

"I don't understand. Why would he want to track down my grandmother now, years after she wrote to him?"

"He wants to track you down. He's been trying to ever since he received the letter."

"He wants to find me?"

"I think we better get you something to eat and check into the hotel. Then you can figure out what you're going to do when Mr. Maddox reaches out to you."

"What if I don't want him to know? Maybe I don't want anything to do with him."

"I can't help you hide from this. I don't want to hurt you, but the man deserves to know his child is alive, safe, and brilliant. It's not his fault he was cut out of your life. But that doesn't mean you have to agree to have any kind of relationship with him. It's up to you."

Hailey couldn't comprehend what she had just heard. Not only did she have a living father, but he was a successful man that had served his country for twenty years and when given the information, searched for her. No one had ever wanted her beside her grandmother and Finn. How could any of this be real?

✕

DISCOVERING FINN'S CASE involved searching for her put a

big damper on their romantic getaway, and they drove back to Alexandria first thing the next morning. It was as if someone had instantly constructed a huge brick wall between them. She was restless and annoyed with him, or the situation, or both. The car ride was quiet and awkward. Then once they arrived at her place, she just wanted to be alone.

"I realize this isn't your fault, but I just need time to get my thoughts in order," she said, still sitting in the passenger seat.

"I understand," he said.

She avoided looking in his eyes as she collected her bag. His tenderness wasn't what she wanted right now. She wanted to punch something. The realization that someone like Maddox could be her biological father, and he might have wanted her, left her feeling angry with her mother and grandmother for never telling her about him. At the same time, she didn't think she had the capacity to start over with a parent at this age. All those years, wishing someone wanted her or would save her had turned her heart to stone.

"I just have one request," she said. "Can you wait to tell Maddox until after the partners announce who they're selecting for junior partner?" Hailey asked, fighting the emotions that were building up inside.

"Why?"

"Because Baxter is friends with Maddox, and I don't want it to sway his vote. I want to know if I earned this partnership on my own."

Finn nodded. "Okay, I'll inform Maddox after they announce who the new junior partner is tomorrow."

"Thank you."

His hand reached for hers, but she turned to open her door and got out. If he touched her, she would fall apart, and then she wouldn't have the space she needed to think.

Finn got out of the car and pulled her bag from the trunk. Thoughtful and chivalrous as always, he walked her to the door of her building.

"I'll see you in the morning then?" he asked and kissed her cheek.

Holding back tears, she nodded and accepted the bag from him before escaping inside and running up her stairs.

As soon as she was in her apartment, the big fat tears rolled down her cheeks, and even though she craved the ability to turn to Finn and let him help her, she was too used to dealing with life's curveballs alone. And this was the biggest one yet.

Chapter Seventeen

Finn

ALTHOUGH IT TOOK every ounce of his strength to drive away from Hailey, it was clear she needed to be alone. He couldn't imagine what it would feel like to learn you might have a parent that never knew about you, and one that could have protected you from all the horrible things you went through in life. If he had to guess, she was in flight mode and would run scared. But he didn't know where that would leave him.

The next morning, one of Baxter's assistants greeted him as soon as he arrived at his desk and told him to be in the conference room at nine a.m. Hailey was already in her office, but he knew she wanted to maintain the professional lines, so he didn't invade her space. Instead he texted her.

Good morning, I hope you got a good night's sleep. I think you're about to get a big caseload dumped on you.

We'll see.

Each of the ten senior partners were in the conference room waiting for them when they arrived, and there was a large spread of breakfast items on the conference table like a celebratory feast, along with a champagne tower and coffee in silver carafes.

"Finn and Hailey, you delivered on the Tovar case, both proving you could put the firm and your client's needs first. You won the case and worked as a team. Each of you possess the qualities we seek in our junior partners, and we hope you'll both stay once we announce our decision," Baxter said.

Mrs. Stewart stepped forward, and Finn smiled knowing they'd made the right decision.

"Hailey Adams, congratulations on being selected as the new junior partner at Baxter and Stewart. We hope you'll accept this offer." Mrs. Stewart held out her hand to Hailey.

Finn turned to see the initial shock and awe on Hailey's face, the elation of success after years of work quickly replaced by a polite smile. Stepping forward, she shook Mrs. Stewart's hand.

"Thank you, I accept. I have to say, Finn was the ideal teammate."

The group cheered, and he couldn't help but beam at her success. He wanted to hug her but didn't risk upsetting her carefully established lines at work. After the festivities, she disappeared into Mrs. Stewart's office, and he decided to take advantage of the moment to meet with Baxter alone to turn in his resignation.

"Sir, no hard feelings at all, but I think I underestimated how much I'd miss the Navy, and I wanted to let you know I plan to meet with JAG about a new commission."

Baxter shook his hand. "I admit I wondered if you were ready to settle into corporate law or needed to practice law with a bit more grit. I support you one hundred percent."

"I think JAG will be a great place to figure that out," Finn said.

"I agree, but there will always be a desk for you in the rookie bullpen if you change your mind. I'm happy to write you a recommendation letter and speak to anyone over there," Mr. Baxter said.

"I'll finish out my current caseload before I make any moves. I have an update for Admiral Maddox. I'm just waiting for him to phone me back."

"I appreciate that, Finn. I hope you can help him find some kind of closure."

There was no need for him to out Hailey as Maddox's heir. It was up to the two of them on who they wanted to know and when.

The rest of the day, he only saw Hailey once, when she returned to the rookie bullpen to retrieve her few things and move up to an office on the partner floor.

Several of the rookies congratulated her, and their tones were already more reverent with a tinge of nervousness. He managed to catch her eye briefly, but she was all business. Now she'd had two major life changes in less than thirty-six hours, so he was going to try to give her the space if she needed it.

Maddox phoned him back and they had a decent conversation about what Finn had learned, and he was honest in telling him that Hailey knew and had made partner. He cautioned Maddox to let Hailey decide when she was ready to meet. Maddox was appreciative and stunned to know he had already seen his own daughter and not realized it. He thanked Finn and said he would give Hailey time and space but asked that all of his inheritances be drafted with her as his sole heir.

×

BY SUNDAY AFTERNOON, his patience was wearing thin. Although she'd responded to his texts, Hailey was clear she needed more time to absorb everything that was going on. He hadn't even had a chance to tell her he was resigning, but he assumed she would be relieved. There was no reason they couldn't be together now.

Restlessness had him driving to his parents' house well before the traditional family dinner. His mom was at the farmers' market but he found his dad out back, attempting to train his attack dog, Biffy, using a pillowcase filled with straw as the target. The small white fuzz ball looked confused and unimpressed.

"Dad, do you really think she can stop an intruder?"

"Care to be a live test dummy?" his dad asked with too much enthusiasm before giving him a big hug.

"No chance, the last thing I need is stitches from a powder puff."

Leading Finn up to the back porch, his dad refilled Biffy's water bowl and had a seat.

"What brings you over so early? Shouldn't you be out to brunch with Hailey?"

Finn sat and joined his dad in the shade.

"It's complicated." Finn sighed.

"I take it you mean your relationship with Hailey?"

He nodded. Of course his folks knew he was interested in Hailey the moment he'd introduced her. Not only because he'd never brought another woman home, but it was impossible for him not to gush about her. He'd filled them in on her background too.

"Hailey seemed to have a sordid past, not of her own making, but in my experience, a person doesn't just move on from trauma. It forms the way they view relationships, and their place in the world. You've seen that with your own teammates," his dad said.

"I know, and just like war trauma, she needs to be ready to deal with it on her own time. The thing is, I think she just needs to accept how far she's come and what she's accomplished. She's been grinding it out so long, she doesn't recognize she's already made it. Even now, after she won the partnership."

"Or maybe, actually achieving this long-running difficult goal is unsettling for her. She identifies as the underdog, and now she is the top dog."

"I thought Mom was the deep one," Finn said, blown away by his father's ability to see things so clearly.

"Nah, she gets all her good material from me." His dad smiled. "So what can you do?"

"Be patient and wait?"

"Or keep moving forward with your own goals and see if she comes around. You've been debating about going back to the Navy. What about the junior partnership? Were you ever going to accept that if you did win it?"

"No, my heart isn't in private sector law, as good as the money is. I have a meeting with the Navy JAG later this week. They're going to spell out my options."

His dad nodded. "Son, when you returned from every mission, it was like sadness had seeped into your eyes. Your mom and I were always terrified it would swallow you up, but here you are. Five years out, and we haven't seen that sadness again until we met Hailey. Don't get me wrong, she's smart and sweet, but her heartaches are still with her. She may need a lot more time to come to terms with them. She may never believe she deserves the kind of love and family you're willing to give her."

Leaning forward, Finn let his father's words settle around him. He knew his dad was right. So many of his fellow soldiers went to war and never returned, while others made it back but couldn't move beyond the trauma. He couldn't fix things for Hailey. He couldn't even love away her pain.

"So you're saying I shouldn't tiptoe around Hailey's pain or try to help her?"

"No, I'm saying tell her exactly how you feel and what you want in a partner. And be prepared for her not to be ready, ever."

"That's got heartbreak written all over it," Finn said.

"You wouldn't be the first man to love a woman into believing she deserved everything her heart didn't dare to trust."

"I don't want to lose her."

His dad's strong hand landed on his shoulder in a comforting grip.

"I know you don't, but that's part of loving someone through the good and the bad."

Finn had been avoiding that word ever since Hailey let him kiss her, but it rang true. He did love her, and if she wasn't ready to let him, then he'd better get on with the pain.

On Monday, after a long day of triaging what needed to

get done and more avoidance from Hailey, Finn stood outside her apartment door. He knew she was busy at work and there was now an invisible line between them because she was the managing partner of the rookies and he was still a rookie, but he'd expected more from her. They hadn't had a chance to speak privately at all, and he was worried about what was going through her head. She must still be reeling from all the new pressure of the partnership and potentially had spoken with Maddox, but he needed to tell her his plan to resign.

Admittedly, he would choose her over working at Baxter and Stewart, but he didn't want her to think he was resigning because he didn't get partner. JAG felt exactly where he needed to be, and it was possible he could still work out of the Naval command in Washington D.C. And that meant he could still see Hailey all the time if she was still interested.

Now he just needed to tell her how he felt about her and let her decide if there was a place for him in her life.

She buzzed him up and let him into her apartment with a furrowed brow.

"I heard a rumor you were resigning," she said.

"Sorry, I planned to tell you myself, but you were pretty busy today. I want you to know I'm not resigning because I think I deserved it over you."

"Okay, then why?"

"I've said from the beginning, they would be foolish not to select you. I never doubted you were the next junior partner."

"Does that mean you're going back to the Navy? Because I'm not sure where that leaves us," she said.

"I love you," he blurted out, surprising them both.

"Wait, what? No, you don't. You barely know me."

"That's not entirely true. I know I miss you when we're apart. I worry if someone will catch your eye or be unkind to you. I know you make my heart pound and my hands itch with wanting to touch you. For two years, I've admired you and fought every desire to be close to you because I didn't know how. You inspire me and challenge me. And I wonder if our kids will have blue or green eyes? Which can only mean one thing…"

"You have weird thoughts?"

"I have been interested in you since my first day at the firm when you told another rookie that if they didn't understand the legal system favored the law breakers they were in the wrong profession." He risked taking a step closer and gripped her shaking hand in his. "I fell in love with you over legal briefs, and I want to be together, for real."

"That sounds very domestic and probably normal in the course of a relationship, like how you're used to seeing your siblings settle down. Next, they'll all have kids and live happily ever after."

He smiled because there was a *but* coming.

"But I'm not from that world. I don't know how to do that, and I've never wanted it."

"How do you know if you've never let yourself believe you could have it?"

Backing away, she put space between them.

"Don't do that. Don't try to get into my head. I know what I want. I want the stability of being a partner at the firm, and I finally got it. Now I know I can depend on myself and the firm."

"I'm not trying to get in your head, only your heart. I understand your tunnel vision focus on your career security has been a driving force, but what about love?"

"I know what I'm capable of and what I want. Love isn't a part of that equation, Finn," she said. "I don't dream of happily-ever-afters and a house with kids running around. I'm not the girl for you."

"So for the next fifty years, you'll work as the best lawyer in D.C. and what?" Finn stepped closer urging her to not look away. "When you're old and gray, who will be sitting beside you? Are you surrounded by grandkids? Or more cats and the love of your life?"

"I've only ever seen myself in my future. The one person I can count on. And now you and Maddox are trying to rewrite my little life."

"Will you at least consider the idea of being with me? Not hiding from how you feel. We can start fresh with a real relationship where we don't have to hide or steal moments together. Let me love you and just see where it might lead us."

She shook her head, and her eyes blinked rapidly.

"No, I have too much going on right now. And I can't be with you and then watch you go off to war and then just wait for bad news."

"I don't think the Navy will send their litigators out to the front line."

"But you don't know, and we both know the Navy will do what it has to do."

"Technically, they could, but I'll be working in D.C.,

unless I request a different assignment."

"How can you be sure?"

"Nothing in life is a guarantee. Instead of looking for excuses, consider what we could create together. Admit to yourself that you have feelings for me, that you're invested in this relationship, that you'll claim me and be open to a future together."

Hailey stood a foot away from him with her lips parted and her topaz-blue eyes filling with tears as she stared at him. She looked terrified, and he almost felt bad asking her to make a commitment, but he needed her to be ready to take the leap with him. Closing the final step between them, he took both her hands in his and placed one gentle kiss on her lips.

"I love you. Can you let yourself love me back?"

One tear slid down her cheek before she swiped at it and stepped several feet away.

"This is exactly why I didn't want to start anything with someone I work with. It's always complicated. What if you resent me for quitting the firm or get sent on a mission and killed? It will be my fault."

"I didn't quit for you. The Navy is where I belong. Those are just excuses."

Shaking her head, she swiped at her eyes as more tears formed.

"Dig deep, babe, and be honest with yourself. Can you see a future with me? Can you put yourself out there? Because even if I'm not in the Navy, life can be fleeting. Here one day and gone the next. But I will love you every single day."

Gulping in air as she started to sob, Hailey turned away from him. It wasn't the answer he wanted, but she wasn't ready.

"Call me when you're ready to talk about us." He left before he got down on his knees and begged.

Chapter Eighteen

Hailey

THE MAN TOLD her he loved her and wanted a future with her, and she freaked out in epic style.

To be fair, she never even let herself consider a future beyond her law career until Finn worked his way into her life. Pushing her at every turn, then he quits his job and professes his love for her the same week she finds out her biological dad she never knew existed wants a relationship with her.

What did he expect? Any cornered wild animal would get defensive.

Sitting on the floor of her living room with her cat staring at her like she was insane, she emptied a box of tissues to wipe up her tears as a knot lodged in her throat. Stifling fear sat heavy over her. She knew what she wanted, and she knew what was holding her back, as if she was stuck in chains. She was terrified to love Finn because losing someone was more painful than never having them.

Alone was where she thrived—count on no one, answer to no one. And then Finn happened with his sexy muscles, keen mind, and sweet, protective nature. She thought she could compartmentalize him, keep it casual, but it snowballed fast into a full-on emotional connection and chemistry that was off the charts. In reality, it was already too late. Even if she never saw him again, she already cared too much about him. Her heart felt cracked open when he left. But what if she did take a chance on Finn and threw caution to the wind? If for some reason it didn't work out or he was deployed by the Navy and killed in action, could she survive that?

Wasn't it safer to end things now before she got too far gone? Stick with her status quo alone where no one could hurt her?

×

THE REST OF the week went by in a blur of new cases, managing the rookies and their caseloads, and avoiding Finn. Because no matter how much she wanted to fall into his arms, she couldn't be so vulnerable at work. She was learning how to be a junior partner, while managing her own caseload and the seven rookie lawyers. On Wednesday, she received a certified letter stating she was Admiral Maddox's sole heir with a copy of his will, and she broke down in tears in her office. The man had already bequeathed her his life's work, and she hadn't even spoken to him yet. She'd responded to his first attempt to contact her with one short email saying she was aware of the possibility he could be her biological father, and that she wasn't ready to deal with it. It had been cold but also all she could muster.

Now a week after learning she was his child, he'd left her

his fortune, his name, and his life's work. How could she have gone from having no one to having a father and a man like Finn professing his love for her?

After Finn's visit to her place, there had been no calls, no texts, no emails. He was giving her the space she demanded. And it was forcing her to keep busy, so her apartment was spotless and she'd gone to the gym every evening, looking for someone to spar with.

In desperation to find out what kind of man Maddox was, she agreed to meet him for dinner. They were meeting at seven that night at a fancy Michelin-star restaurant, and she had no idea what to expect. She'd stayed at the office late, reading up on several new cases she was assigned and planned to use the firm's car service, a nice perk of the partnership. She had no idea what to expect. Her nerves were shot, and she wished she could call Finn to speak with him about what to say to her dad. But it wouldn't be fair to reject him and then expect his help.

As if he could read her thoughts—or they were connected by some invisible thread—her phone chimed with a text from him before she left her office.

I miss you. I know you have a lot going on. If you need me, I'm always on your side.

Tears welled in her eyes, and she collapsed back into her seat at her desk. She didn't want any of it and wanted all of it at the same time. She wanted to meet her father and yell at him for leaving her in foster care. She wanted to accept Finn's love and hope they could turn it into something real and lasting. But would it all upset the safe life she worked so hard to create? Finally, her life was stable and in order, and these two men threatened to overturn everything. What if she took a chance on them, and they destroyed her, just like her mom?

At one minute after seven, she walked through the dimly lit restaurant, where she heard it took months to get a reservation in.

"Ms. Adams?" The maitre d' asked with a pinched look on his face. Before she could respond, he cut her off. "This way. Mr. Maddox reserved a private room to meet you. You're quite young to be a lawyer."

She was surprised the man knew that.

He ushered her down an opulent hallway lined with wine bottles in glass cases, each labeled with Roman numerals and locks. He knocked on a wood door before opening it to reveal a generous room with a table set for two, a wood burning fireplace, and Admiral Maddox, who stood to greet her.

"Ah, Ms. Adams, thank you for agreeing to meet over dinner," he said, then nodded to the maitre d' who took his leave.

"Why did you tell him I was your lawyer?" she asked, starting to feel cornered.

Maddox heaved a sigh. "Everyone in this town gossips, and they'll think you're my date if I don't give them a reason I'm meeting a beautiful young woman for dinner."

"Oh."

"I didn't think you'd like me to name you as my daughter and sole heir just yet." His smile was bashful and kind at the same time, instantly putting her at ease.

"No," she admitted.

He smiled and held out a seat for her near the fire, maybe sensing her nerves had her chilled.

"I understand this is all a bit shocking, and I've had years to warm up to the idea you existed. I'm still surprised Finn actually found you and to believe you were right here all this time."

"How long have you known I existed?"

He sat across from her and linked his fingers together before taking a deep breath as if he needed it to prop him up.

"I'm going to tell you everything, and then you can decide if you want anything to do with me." His eyes held hers. "But no matter what you decide, I am leaving you my wealth. You're my blood and although I was robbed of raising you, protecting you, and loving you, you're still mine. I want you to have it and do whatever you want with it."

She gulped the cool water in front of her and nodded.

"I dated your mother one summer before I shipped out with the SEAL teams. She was gorgeous, fun, and didn't take anything seriously. When I said I was leaving on my first mission, she gave me a kiss and said she'd be seeing me, that I should look her up next time I was back. But when I returned, she was already married and living in North Carolina. Life moved on. She never reached out to me, never told me about you. I had no idea she'd died until your grandmother wrote to me."

Hailey's eyes hurt from not blinking, but she was riveted to hear about the young vivacious woman her mom had been. She only had a smattering of memories, and they were mostly all of her being sad or passed out. Taking another big drink of her water, she watched as Maddox unfolded a letter from his suit coat and handed it to her. With eager interest she poured over her grandmother's handwriting and recognized the struggle in the misspelled words and sloppy penmanship.

"She never told me. She must have thought we all had time. Later, she couldn't write or speak well, and then she was gone."

He nodded with a grimace.

"I know. I was out on my last deployment and that letter took four months to find me back in Virginia Beach. I had just retired my commission and started my business."

"Too bad Gran didn't believe in email."

They both laughed, breaking the seriousness of the moment.

"My company was an overnight success, or so it seemed, but I'd tinkered with ideas and tech for years. Anyway I'd just been named a *Fortune 500* company when the letter arrived. I thought it was a crazy scam, but I went to see your gran because her name rang a bell. Your mother went by Bella Ray Burke when I knew her."

"Oh, right, her maiden name."

"I don't think your mom wanted me to find out about you, but your gran invited me to visit if I wanted to know more. I found her at the nursing home, and she didn't seem to understand who I was or remember the letter. I sat with her for a bit, read to her, and saw one picture of your mother. I knew it was all true. I knew then I had a little girl out there somewhere, and I've been looking ever since."

Tears clouded Hailey's eyes and she stubbornly swiped at them, but it was useless.

"I'm not usually a crier."

His eyes were misted over and it looked like he wanted to reach out to her, but he hesitated.

"Me either, but I think we're allowed some leniency."

She smiled and used her napkin to wipe her wet cheeks.

"I don't understand why she never told me."

"I'm guessing she didn't know from the beginning. Maybe your mom left something behind that your gran discovered later."

"We'll probably never know," Hailey said.

"I visited her a few more times, but one day, they said your gran had passed away. When I asked to go through her things, they said her relative had already picked it up. They wouldn't give me any information about you. I must have only missed you by a few days."

"I was in law school at the time, and it was a really hard time. There've been a lot of hard times, and it just seems crazy to find out now you were out there all this time."

"I would have saved you all of that pain if I had known, Hailey. I would have loved you and protected you."

She shook her head. "I believe you. I don't need you to make any amends or feel guilty about what happened. It was my mom's fault. You don't have to leave me your life's work."

He shook his head a moment, but then his blue eyes filled with tears.

"It's not from guilt so much as pride. It's hard to explain, but the minute I knew you existed, I fell in love with the idea of having you. I've focused so much on my career I never stopped to think about what it's all for, who I can share a holiday with, maybe go golfing or surfing or whatever you like to do. You're my daughter, and I would really like to know you. And I admit I'm angry we were robbed of twenty-eight years together. You had to do so much on your own. But I don't want you to ever worry another day in your life. You'll have money, security, and me if you want to. It's the least I can do."

Hailey let out a breath she didn't know she was holding. "I'm not any good at accepting handouts or help."

He laughed. "Well, you may get that from me and your mom."

"I want to be mad at her, but I also want to know everything you know about her."

"Your mom was the kind of personality that took over a room, a free spirit no one could catch and everyone wanted to be with."

Three hours later and many more tears, Hailey agreed to see her father again that weekend. He congratulated her on her promotion and told her over and over how proud he was of her. They hugged when she finally said good night, and on the ride home in a taxi, she felt like a huge weight had been lifted off her shoulders. Meeting her dad suddenly grounded her on the planet, but she ached to share it with Finn.

Lying in bed that night, she wondered what he was doing. Every inch of her body wanted to jump out of bed and go find him. Her heart yearned to talk to him, but she held back. What if she wasn't capable of loving him the way he deserved? What if he changed his mind, and she was stuck the rest of her life with a broken heart?

But it felt like her heart was already breaking. Her dad had said something that seemed directed at her when he said he'd been so focused on the mission while in the Navy, he forgot to have a life and a family. He'd realized too late how much he missed out on.

Whipping back the covers, she didn't even bother to change. She just shoved her feet into some sneakers and grabbed her keys. It was late, but she could always find a cab at the corner taxi stand. She opened her door, and a large fresh bouquet of pink daisies sat on her doormat.

She took the steps two at a time down the stairs and burst outside the door to find Finn getting into his car.

"Babe," she yelled, and his head popped up. Closing the door, he met her on the sidewalk as she hurtled herself into his arms. Warm soothing hands ran over her back before he lifted her off her feet in a hug that felt intimate and intoxicating. His mouth settled in her hair by her ear. "Did you just call me babe?" he asked.

"Yes. I was just going to storm over to your place, and here you are."

"Because of the flowers?"

"No, because I am ridiculously in love with you and trying to resist gravity is futile."

His mouth was on hers and his hand slid up her back behind her neck to cradle her head. She could feel a smile spread on his mouth.

"Those flowers worked even better than I'd hoped," he said, lifting her up off her feet again.

Still holding the pink flowers while her arms were wrapped around his neck, she gave him a week's worth of kisses before either of them could speak again.

"I missed you so much," he said.

"I'm sorry it took me so long to figure it all out."

"What did you figure out?"

"That I'm going to love you either way, so I may as well enjoy you, up close and personal. That life is too short to hold back on having everything with you and I don't need to be alone or prove I can do it all myself anymore. I don't even want to do it all myself anymore."

"Emm, my baby is so smart," Finn said.

"I love you."

"I love you more, and I'm about to show you all night," he said before swooping her up in his arms and carrying her back up the stairs. True to his word, Finn loved her into blissful oblivion. They took turns kissing away the doubts, and Hailey knew she met her match with Finn. He was her one and only.

Chapter Nineteen

Finn

A MONTH AFTER resigning from the firm, Finn was dressed in his white Navy uniform and leaving the JAG office at the Naval Command Headquarters in Washington D.C. Hailey was supposed to pick him up, and they were heading out of town for the Fourth of July. They'd been sharing his car and basically living together since they'd made up.

Scanning the street, he didn't see his black sports car and checked his watch. But then a midnight-blue Porsche hummed up to the curb and a familiar gorgeous blonde popped out.

"Hey sailor, need a lift?"

"That depends, whose car did you steal?"

"Maddox lent it to me; said we need something safe to drive in."

Laughing, he got inside.

"Did he say safe or fast?"

"Maybe both." She leaned over for a kiss before maneuvering back into traffic.

"Are you ready for a weekend with all the Maguires?" he

asked.

"Yes, I'm excited to meet your sister. I bet she has the best dirt on you."

"I see, this is a recon trip."

"Are you sure it's not weird if my dad—I mean if Maddox comes down on Saturday?"

"Not weird at all. It's a family weekend."

She nodded as the words settled over her. It was taking her time to get used to the idea of having any family. He hoped she would warm up more to it because he couldn't imagine being without her.

"We've officially been dating for a month," she said, smirking at him.

"No, it's been two months. You're a great lawyer but terrible at math."

"Explain how that works."

"We started dating the night I ran six miles to get you the best Thai food in town, in the rain."

"I thought that was just dinner and work mashed together."

"Yeah, me working on getting you to accept you needed to date me."

×

TWO HOURS LATER, they pulled into the family cabin that was lit up and buzzing with activity. Out in the yard, there were tiki torches lit, kids were running around with sparklers, and someone had music rocking.

"Will we get our room with the bunk beds?" she asked,

reaching her hand over to slide up his thigh.

"Probably the healing room, which is better. More pillows to cover your moans."

"Oh my gosh, is it that bad?"

"No. I love it almost as much as I love you."

Reaching over the center console, he wove his hand in her hair, and her mouth met his halfway. In no time, they had fogged up all the windows.

"We should have made a pit stop before we got here," he said.

"It's not too late to go park somewhere," she breathed.

"Always keep them wanting more," he said and nibbled her lower lip.

"What?" she said, pulling out of his embrace.

"My buddy on the teams said the easiest way to keep your wife happy is to always keep them wanting more."

"Wife?"

He gazed into her lust-filled eyes, then kissed her gingerly.

"I hope you will be one day." He watched as her eyes searched his for the truth, meeting her head-on with it because he loved her and he wanted her forever.

"How do you know I'm the one?"

"Ever since I first saw you, I knew there was something between us. Like a magic spell you cast over me, drawing me in. I'm just waiting for you to catch up."

A blush blossomed in her cheeks, and she fished a key out of her purse and handed it to him. The key was silver with a heavy weight to it and an odd, grooved pattern.

"What's this key for?"

"It's a master key to our new place."

"You took the plunge and bought something? Wait, did you say ours?"

She nodded her head up and down while biting her bottom lip.

"Sort of. I got a brownstone closer to your office instead of that apartment I was looking at. It needs some work, and I thought maybe we could decide on updates together."

"That sounds perfect."

"Are you sure? Because I wanted to surprise you but then realized maybe you would want to help pick out your next home."

"I'll live anywhere with you."

"You really do love me."

"For ever and ever," Finn promised.

~The End.

Epilogue

HAILEY'S PALMS WERE sweating, her nerves were so shot, and this was only the first day of their wedding festivities... What had she been thinking, agreeing to all this? After Finn proposed, she hadn't thought too much about how to plan a wedding until they agreed neither of them wanted a long engagement. Now after dating for a year, they were about to be man and wife, and she didn't have any doubts about it. She wasn't scared to tie herself to Finn forever, or be his wife, but she didn't love the idea of being on display for the ceremony or tonight's rehearsal dinner.

"Babe, are you in here?" Finn's voice called out as she heard their hotel suite door open and close.

Taking a deep breath, she smoothed her white-and-navy striped dress. It was a strapless piece she'd loved in the shop because the top had a flouncy ruffle to it that made her feel feminine, but in the bright light of the bathroom she realized how much it showed her scars.

"Hey, gorgeous, are you almost ready? The boat is here."

Finn appeared behind her in the mirror, and his appreciative gaze took her in. Her blonde hair was curled into soft waves, and she had a tan from their recent weekends at the lake. He stepped farther into the bathroom and pressed his chest against the back of her body as his arms enveloped her.

"This is a nice view." His eyes met hers in the mirror before he kissed her neck.

"I'm worried that maybe this is showing too much… skin."

Reaching in her makeup bag she pulled out some cream she used on occasion to cover some of the bolder scars.

"I don't want to make anyone uncomfortable."

Finn sighed. "Everyone here loves you and only sees your beauty, but if it will make you more comfortable, then do it. I don't want anything to distract you from enjoying the day."

His mouth pressed more kisses over her shoulder and collarbone, and she could feel the stir of arousal between them.

"You're about to distract us both into missing this boat," she said, craning her neck to meet his mouth in a hot, take me now kind of a kiss.

"Maybe we can borrow a paddleboard and catch up to them later," Finn said.

His hands spun her toward him, and he slowly pulled up the hem of her skirt before lifting her up onto the bathroom counter.

"We're going to be late, and everyone will know why," she breathed as she undid his belt and her knees rose to frame his abs.

"Ask me if I care later." With one swift motion, he was buried deep inside her, and all her self-conscious worries floated away as Finn loved her into orgasmic bliss.

Thirty minutes later, they were both freshened up, and

she was only worried about her mussed hair and the bright pink blush in her cheeks when they finally arrived on the pier. There was a large seventy-four-foot sailboat waiting with all their closest friends and family for them. Luckily, the music was playing, and everyone seemed to be having a grand time before they even set sail.

"The bride and groom are finally here. We can set sail. Shiver me timbers," Conner yelled to the crowd, receiving a boisterous response.

Finn helped her up the steps, and she easily found her sea legs on such a large boat.

Finn's mom hugged her first. "Hello, my soon-to-be brilliant daughter-in-law. You look ravishing. A little time out of the office suits you."

Finn winked at her over his mother's head.

Next, Mr. Maguire pulled her in for a warm hug, and she had to admit she enjoyed their affection. While falling in love with Finn had snuck up on her, falling for his family was a given. All the Maguire kids instantly treated her like one of the family, and she was still shocked a year after meeting Finn to feel so much belonging.

"Hey, kiddo." Her dad, Admiral Maddox, swooped in and put his arm around her shoulder before kissing her forehead.

They had taken their time getting to know each other, but in the end, they were too much alike to deny the connection. And they both seemed as intrigued by the similarities that existed even though she'd grown up without him. They both tilted their heads when considering a dilemma. They both sneezed three times in a row when something tickled their senses. They both loved sardines on pizza and were Scrabble addicts. In fact, games and puzzles were one of the first things they found they had in common. Now every Sunday, she had breakfast with her dad, and they did a crossword or played Scrabble, and in the evenings, he usually joined her and Finn at the Maguires for Sunday dinner. They were a packaged deal.

Everyone was dressed in casual summer dresses, and the men had linen shirts on with shorts. The early June sun was warm, but there was a nice breeze coming off the water along the Chesapeake. They were getting married in Annapolis, Maryland, at the Naval Academy where Finn and her father had both gone to school. It was an honor to use the chapel, and she was happy to be close to the water. It always felt like home, but now, getting married to a Navy officer, it seemed as if it was always meant to be.

"Ahoy," called the captain from the bow of the boat. "If we're all accounted for, we'll be setting sail. Everyone take a seat while the crew prepares the boat, and then we'll let you know when it's safe to move about."

Finn appeared and handed her a plastic glass of bubbly, then led her to their seats clearly marked with *Mr. and Mrs.* signs.

"I like that," she said. "It sounds so official."

"I can't believe it hasn't come up, but did you want to change your name? Or would you rather not? I can totally understand if you don't want to."

He was being shy about asking, but she suspected he would prefer she change her name.

"I actually can't wait to change my name," she said.

Finn's face broke into a big smile. "Really?"

"I was thinking I would change two of my names—Hailey Maddox Maguire."

"Wow, that's a big step, and I think it's fantastic. If you tell your dad now, he's going to need a box of tissues."

"I'll wait until after the wedding. He's really got a lot on his plate, giving away the daughter he never knew."

Finn's deep laugh carried over the wind, and his sister, Charlotte, sitting across from them, beamed.

"You make my brother so happy, Hailey. I only wish he'd found you sooner!" Charlotte said.

"I think we found each other at the exact right time. I mean, I did obsess over her for two years while working at the firm. But she was busy making a name for herself. She needed time to discover me," Finn said.

Charlotte's husband Caleb piped up, "I think that's a woman thing."

Conner nodded as he squeezed his wife Hannah into his side. "Agreed."

"I don't know what you're talking about. I nearly had to drag your brother down the aisle," Ainsley said before kissing Rory's surprised face.

"Woman, you must be hallucinating. I was so madly in love with you I was going to fly to New York every weekend just so we could be together," Rory said.

"Maybe that's fate. We just find our perfect person when the time is right," Hailey said.

Finn captured her lips in another searing kiss, and not even the whoops and cheers could pull her attention away. This man owned her, body and soul, and she couldn't wait to be his wife.

The boat sailed by the Naval Academy and down the Chesapeake, until the captain threw the anchor and announced they could all move around and enjoy the views. It was an intimate crowd with only the Maguires, her father, and several of Finn's teammates.

"This is a nice-sized group. Who else is coming tomorrow?" Ainsley asked, as they each sampled a few of the mini desserts set out.

"Well a few people from the firm, but most of the guests will be from the Maguire family. I didn't realize how many cousins Finn had," Hailey said.

"Oh my gosh, yes. I had no idea either, and since we basically eloped, I didn't experience the full onslaught until the first Fourth of July family weekend at the lake."

"So between his dad's five brothers, they have like twenty cousins, and then on his mom's side, another ten. It's a lot of family," Hailey said.

"It will make for a fun event though, they're all so beautiful too, like an oddly 'everyone is gorgeous' family," Ainsley said, looking over at her husband standing with Charlotte, Conner, and Finn.

Hailey laughed. "You're no slouch either, Mrs. Ainsley Maguire."

"I guess that means these babies will be adorable," Ainsley whispered.

"Babies, as in multiple?"

"Yes, I also didn't realize twins ran in the Maguire family genes until Charlotte mentioned it."

"What did I mention?" she said, joining them and eyeing

a mini éclair. "Oh, I ate so many of these when I was pregnant."

Hailey stuffed hers in her mouth so she wouldn't say the wrong thing.

"Well, that must run in the genes too."

"What?" Charlotte said, looking between them. "Wait, are you pregnant?" she whisper-yelled at Ainsley.

Ainsley shoved the second small donut in her mouth and nodded, causing Charlotte to jump up and down with glee.

"I just love having sisters. Hailey, I hope you don't mind the idea of an older, attentive, sister that wants to have sleepovers and spa playdates."

Before Hailey could reply, Hannah walked up and encircled Hailey's waist. "Is everyone excited for our sleepover tonight? It's a tradition for your last night as a single woman," Hannah said.

"I'm looking forward to hearing all your tips on being a good wife," Hailey said.

"Oh, I'll have to think of something other than let him spoil you and don't start doing his laundry. That last bit was something my mom said," Ainsley said. "At first I thought she was being rude, but she was right."

Hailey laughed, but Hannah and Charlotte nodded.

"Excuse me, ladies, but I believe I get a little more time with my bride before your hen night commences," Finn said, walking over and slipping his hand in hers.

He led her to the front of the boat and the setting sun cast a burnt-orange glow around him.

"Once they fall asleep, you can sneak back into our room," he said between kisses on her face.

She nodded. "Okay, I didn't have the heart to tell them I don't want to spend one last night away from you. They're all so excited to have a sleepover."

"They talk a big game, but I bet every single one of them will be back in their own beds before the night is over."

Hailey laughed and hugged her arms around his neck, loving the strength he exuded. "What's that they say about too much of a good thing?"

"Oh, I don't believe I could ever get enough of you, but I'm willing to spend the rest of our lives trying." His smiling lips pressed against hers, and she knew without a shadow of a doubt she would never get enough of him and she was totally okay with that. Being with Finn and becoming a Maguire was exactly where she was always meant to be.

~The Real End

If you enjoyed *Love and Order,*
you'll love the next book in the…

Legacy of the Maguires series

Book 1: *Last First Kiss*

Book 2: *Battle of Hearts*

Book 3: *Strictly Off Limits*

Book 4: *Love and Order*

Book 5: Coming soon!

Available now at your favorite online retailer!

About the Author

Author of your next binge-worthy romance series, Stella has been plotting sexy, tear-jerker stories since she was old enough to hold a pencil. Born a Georgia peach, Stella loves all things country but calls the beach home even though she's currently living outside D.C. with her family. Most days she can be found drinking too much coffee, collecting lipstick she forgets to wear, and baking.

Thank you for reading

Love and Order

If you enjoyed this book, you can find more from all our great authors at TulePublishing.com, or from your favorite online retailer.

CPSIA information can be obtained
at www.ICGtesting.com
Printed in the USA
JSHW020052160723
44666JS00001B/48

9 781959 988854